T0319205

Died Not Dead

Nfor Ngala Nfor

Langaa Research & Publishing CIG
Mankon, Bamenda

Publisher:

Langaa RPCIG
Langaa Research & Publishing Common Initiative Group
P.O. Box 902 Mankon
Bamenda
North West Region
Cameroon
Langaagrp@gmail.com
www.langaa-rpcig.net

Distributed in and outside N. America by African Books Collective
orders@africanbookscollective.com
www.africanbookscollective.com

ISBN: 9956-763-28-4

© Nfor Ngala Nfor 2016

All rights reserved.
No part of this book may be reproduced or transmitted in any form or by
any means, mechinal or electronic, including photocopying and recording,
or be stored in any information storage or retrieval system, without
written permission from the publisher

DISCLAIMER
All views expressed in this publication are those of the author and do not
necessarily reflect the views of Langaa RPCIG.

Chapter One

Eeee! Laye! Laye! Laye! Laye!
    Mu mo a bi mu e! Mu mo a bi mu e!! Mu mo a bi mu e!!!

Competing shrill voices from three women, rented the still air apart, as they emerged from the house with music both on their lips and their feet. The rays of the bright sun shone on their faces and the great joy on their hearts could be seen on their magnetising feminine smiles. From the message conveyed by Laye, accompanied by rhythmic foot movement, every heart was filled with joy for the birth of a first born child into the family. The young girl married into the Royal family had proven her innocence, uprightness and fidelity. The anxiety which had gripped everyone and held every heart in suspense for three days and three nights was now over.

Outside, the number of women singing and dancing was swelling geometrically. But, as usual, all anxious men eager to know the sex of the child were held in check until they had given a present. It was like kindling the appetite of a starved man and thereafter dangling the nutritious food before his very eyes. In Nyamngong it was in moments like this that feminine tyranny goes unchallenged. And they do it with magnetising cheerfulness which in joy attracts anxious and inquisitive men rather than distracts.

This was the beginning of the celebration of the birth of a *mu-rkong*. This male child was the first fruit of the young couple. This attracts special joy and celebration for the newly wedded girl has proved her innocence and purity. The celebration spanned all of the eight-day week. A bevy of women danced from house to house, compound to compound, emitting joy and happiness to all and sundry. A

1

team of women was quickly dispatched with the good news to do the twenty-miles distance to inform the grandfather, Ta Fai Ndingah Nwenfu, the ruler of Tambang clan and second in command in the Kingdom of Nyamngong. Like the angels who bore the news of the birth of Christ to the shepherds, these emissaries proclaimed the good news in songs and dancing to any they met and in every compound they passed and they were welcomed with gifts. A child is possessed by one person when in the womb but belongs to the entire community once he is born.

From the first day Njemucharr was born relations, friends and well-wishers streamed in from all over the kingdom with gifts and presents of different kinds: coins, kola nuts, sweet palm wine, dried leaves of tobacco tied in balls, red palm-oil, castor oil, native salt, meat, *warr, nkwie*, and other condiments. The celebrations were unequaled. Though feasting child birth is women's affairs and tradition forbids men to eat food prepared in a born- house until after one week, men celebrated the birth of Njemucharr in their own way. All had something to talk about, eat, drink, and share in the joy of life after the three nightmarish weary long nights and days.

The family background of the parents had so much to do with the prestige the young boy had from birth. This nevertheless was only in reference to the celebration; for the Nyamngong measure a person's worth by his character and achievements in life which impact the society in general. To the Nyamngong a greedy wealthy man is worthless and of no consequence to the society. He is greatly despised and talked ill of even in songs.

A strong factor to this overwhelming joy was the circumstance of his birth. Kwimnchep, the young mother, had lain groaning for three long and weary days and nights. Anxiety and apprehension was justifiably high for this was her first delivery. Local midwives, some of whom had attained their menopause and had delivered many such delicate cases in the past, explored their skills and experiences to the limit but without success.

At night the groans were unbearable. Everyone in the compound kept vigil. The house in which she lay was parked full with women who all sat in a mournful mood. The conversations were hushed. Men on their part combed the sorcerers' houses to establish the cause, and determine what must be done. Once and again an elder woman would appeal to the men not sit down doing nothing. Every sorcerer the men visited had the same message 'a great gift is on the way'. But the conclusion –'a mist is clouding my views'-- confused the men and caused the anxiety which gripped even the optimist and most devout sorcery consultants.

Mama Njuh, her mother, who had come to welcome her grandchild, sat gazing to the west. She was weak and heavy with sleep. But uppermost and overbearing in her mind was her daughter's fate. The smoke from the life coal she had put in the pipe was getting thinner and thinner. Her mouth had gone dead and dry, even of spit as if a rat had died in her mouth. She could no more cultivate the taste to smoke her tobacco pipe, the only thing that sent her to bed and woke her from sleep. She ploughed into her past and seeing no dent she protested vehemently.

'My in-laws I gave my daughter to you with a clean heart. I held back nothing; I brought her to you innocent and upright having known no man. *'Maluwa,'* she addressed Ma Ndabu 'for this according to our tradition you made me proud. Do our people not say that if the right hand washes the left, the left should do likewise to the right? My husband, as all of you know, is an upright and honest person. He does not drink wine from here and from there. If you people try to do anything

3

wrong with my daughter', her voice sounded hoarse and louder, 'so that you put on our heads, Nyu will not permit such evil intent to happen. I have given birth to twelve; but no one's sleep has ever been disturbed on account that I was in labour. Why should my daughter, my only daughter, suffer this agony? Whoever is blocking the way should remove his or her hand!'

She paused, looking intently into space as if watching the hand removed and the grandchild born instantly. 'Nyu I am in your hands, let me not become a laughing stock before my enemies!' She prayed earnestly, with her hands lifted in supplication towards the heavens.

'I am with you' said Ma Ndabu, tapping her foot gently on the ground. 'It is not you, it is me they want to destroy as if fate has not had enough of me' she said lamentably with her head bowed and shaking gravely from side to side.

Despite the anxiety which had gripped everyone in the entire Royal family and beyond, the grandfather, HRH the Nyamndom, remained calm, sure that the child would be born hale and hearty at the appointed time. The statement did not come as a surprise, since tradition forbids HRH the Nyamndom from expressing horror and anxiety publicly or from exhibiting signs of depression.

Nformi Birr, the husband and would- be young father, on his part, characteristic of his nature, remained calm, confident and optimistic. In his cool epigrammatic manner, he reminded his sympathizers that no known mortal has ever hastened sunrise.

As soon as Ta Fai Ndingah Nwenfu received word about the grave condition of his daughter from his wife, Mama Njuh, he immediately dispatched Ta Nwenchep. At sun rise on the third day he arrived.

'Ta Nwenchep, you are welcome. Thanks to Nyu that you have met me alive, said Ma Ndabu, welcoming Ta Nwenchep whose arrival was in reality a candle of hope.

'Welcome father of our children,' quipped an anxious Mama Njuh.

'Where is she?' demanded Ta Nwenchep, as he hung his sheath machete and ancient leather bag. 'When one's life is on the edge of a razor, there is no time for traditional lengthy greetings,' he remarked paying little attention to greetings from the many around.

'There she is, groaning like a wounded animal. For three days running, who has had a wink? Here is my pipe, cold as ice. See my eyes red and swollen. See my hands; has water touched them?' Mama Njuh complained dramatically.

'She will soon be all right' he said with an air of unquestionable authority as one who had the mandate from the gods to give hope where there is despair and to restore life where death had knocked.

From his ancient goatskin bag he removed three reddish cowries, shook them in his hands and after reciting some incantations he threw them methodically on the floor. He watched them curiously, tapped his index finger on the floor three times and adjusted his stool. After the third throw, he nodded his head three times, picked up the cowries and put them into his bag. As he did this, the men seated watched keenly but understood nothing 'This child is a special child. Let there be no panic,' he pronounced authoritatively.

The men sitting looked at each other in suppressed anxiety.

'You mean to say all will be alright?' asked Gwei.

'Yes. But before he is born, special sacrifices have to be made.' he declared.

'What is a sacrifice compared to human life? What do you need? Tell us!'

5

Bring a black spotless hen that had yet laid no egg, a spotless white cock, '*mbar-ngong*' and three dried rats and three calabashes of fresh palm wine. All these were brought instantly.

In performing the sacrifices, Ta Nwenchep, cut each rat into three pieces, poured cold palm oil into the '*mbar-ngong*' and mixed all the lots together. He brought out one of the abdomens and cut it into four smaller pieces throwing each piece to each of the four corners of the bamboo house that had long been smoked black. As he did this, his lips moved rhythmically, his eyes wide open and without a blink.

In Ma Ndabu's house, Kwimnchep's groaning was giving way to normal labour pains. Her pale patched lips and wrinkled agony face was coming back to life. She demanded for water and three bowls came from three different women all at once. There was now a ray of hope, for in the past two days, she had taken neither food, water nor made any sensible statement. The only sign of life still in her was her ability to groan, and bite the lips. The three women constantly by her bed found it difficult keeping her steady in bed. It was a disturbing experience never had in the family before.

The third stage was the sacrificing of the white cock. As for the hen, it was declared a life sacrifice belonging to the would-be born child. The sacrifice of the cork was the most solemn omen. Ta Nwenchep stood reverently, cock in hand, but without a knife. After murmuring some words, which he alone amongst the mortals present understood, he tore open the beak of the white cock and instantly the cry of the baby was heard. Without twisting or slitting the neck, the cock became cold dead when it dropped to the floor. Thus the dropping of the dead cock matched in contrast with the cry of the baby that announced new life. This was instantly echoed to humanity by the rhythmic life feet and rhythmic voices in sweet music that proclaimed the birth of a *'mu rkong'*.

Ta Nwenchep immunized the baby making him impervious against all human evil machinations. Nformi Birr was specifically told that the first outing of the baby should be to the Nyamngai. The mother was strongly warned not to express anxiety whenever she noticed any extra ordinary behaviour or development from the child. 'Whatever you see or notice, know that it is according to the will of Nyu- Ngong who has sent him, a special gift, to us. My daughter-in-law, note it but keep your lips sealed.' he concluded.

Ta Nwenchep, though at the time was gradually becoming incapacitated by poor sight, was a gynecologist in his own right. Any pregnant woman under labour or any sick child he rejected was like a doctor certifying a patient dead.

The birth of Njemucharr gave people an opportunity to relax, a kind of public holiday. Good enough, it came in between planting and weeding, when there was not so much work. This gave the celebrants the opportunity to celebrate in grand style and the ideal opportunity for jokes about the child.

The soothsayer proclaimed as the best throughout the kingdom and beyond, claimed he had predicted the birth of such a child two years three months ago. This was before the mother became a grown up girl ready for marriage. Tantoh Ncham Ncham said he had made the prediction only to a few men of the land for fear that, if openly made known to many, the witches and wizards would not allow the child to complete his circle in the mother's womb let alone be born. 'Envy is not dead in our land!' he remarked regrettably.

Tantoh Ncham Ncham trudged into the bamboo house where the child was, with the dignity of one who needed no introduction. As he put his right foot on the elevated door step the two small bells jingled, announcing his presence and the

7

women moved back. The newly married women who according to him were daughters- in- law moved respectable distance away. The young girls who could not bear the pungent smell of different leaves and mixtures, his old traditional bag, and his old black clothes, dashed out with sighs, murmuring and hissing laughter. But as for the daughters-in-law, they conducted themselves properly. Tradition forbids that they manifest any disrespectful behaviour in the presence of a father-in-law.

He opened the baby-boy's right hand and nodded his head thrice as if to confirm what he had anticipated. Njemucharr! Njemucharr! Njemucharr! He called three times with his fading brown but penetrating eyes fixed on the boy's tender face. While he made this call, the women stooped, except the very old ones who sat on old bamboo chairs, in grave silence as if expecting a mighty word from the tender lips. A word from babe Njemucharr would only have accorded the women an opportunity to relate the act to another similar wonder, a more spectacular thing Tantoh Ncham Ncham had done in the past.

'Keep the Baby on the ground,' he ordered, his sunken jaws dancing. As he spoke particles of kolanuts already ground spilled from an old black cylindrical object in his left hand and landed exactly on the centre of Njemucharr's lovely face. The elderly woman who had put the boy on bare floor stooped to wipe away the particle, but he ordered her back.

'Ma Boo-Nyu, it is the will of the gods' said Tanto Ncham Ncham proudly. To justify his statement, he inquired whether any stuff fell on any, including the Ma Boo Nyu. All the women, including those far in the dark corners, to confirm their doubts, wiped their faces and examined their palms.

'No!' came the answer like a chorus.

'I have always wondered when women shall begin to reason rightly,' he said mockingly and proudly, startling the women

8

with a quaking laughter. The daughters-in-law whispered their surprise to each other.

'Go ahead Ta Nganchuf', said the eldest woman in the house. 'Do not mind those women', she pleaded exhibiting indifference as if she did not wipe her face also. Because of her age, she was called Mama. She was now the mother, grandmother or great grandmother, depending on the age of those concerned. Though she had lost much of her ability to see, she was the idol of the young children. She would feed them, play with them, and tell them numerous stories about the land, the animal kingdom, birds, some which they will sing, chorus and dance. Mama was a regular centre of attraction, source of inspiration and great entertainer. She would listen tirelessly to the complaints of the children, console and resolve them amicably. Although they were many old women in the house she was the only one married into the Royal family when Tantoh Ncham Ncham was in his early teens; so he could call him by his pet name Nganchuf.

Tantoh Ncham Ncham rubbed his right forefinger on the ground and murmured some magical words and drew a straight line on the boy's fore head. He then asked that the boy be given back to her mother, saying, 'Stay well! I will see you later.' He left the women to join the other men folk inside the palace courtyard. His cylindrical object was in his left palm and with seasoned regularity and precision, he started grinding a lobe.

As he left, the young girls who had forced themselves out, returned each one singing a soft lullaby. Ndapngong was the first to re-enter the house.

'Where is my good husband?' she asked anxiously referring to the new born.

'When you are entering a house always bend down!' screamed an elderly woman. 'You girls of today will show a person wonders. Where is my husband? Where is my good husband? And you forget yourself as to where you are.' she queried.

'Do not mind her. Will she have to wait for him?' asked a nursing mother sitting on the bed and struggling to stop the child crying by putting breast into his mouth.

'Yes do not go and get married wait for your own child to grow and marry you' teased Bongbip.

'All your age-mates and even juniors are either married, expecting a baby or have given birth. Few are yet to move into their husband's houses. But here you are only getting fatter and fatter like a castrated he-goat!' Ndapnjih complemented in her usual jovial manner. At this, all laughed except two: Ndapngong who saw some seriousness in the joke and her mother who, for the past six months, had been getting more and more worried at seeing that her daughter's age-mates were all married. She swallowed a big lump that had suddenly grown in her throat and managed to say that her daughter was married to the church.

All who could sense and read meaning beyond expressed words, knew that the joke went too far. Ndapnjih noted for entertaining jokes, was dreaded for her sarcasms. It was said that, when serious, her jokes struck and gave the afflicted cause for reflection.

Ndapngong contented with the baby in her laps paid no heed to the rest of the things her mothers were saying about her. She sat admiring the baby, indeed every inch of him singing one lullaby or the other. Whenever a man came to the door to greet, she would joyfully and quickly move out with the baby so that no one else would have the opportunity to take the child from her. Such greetings from the men folk came with gifts. Sometimes the women would refuse to show the baby, depending on the social status of the man, until a handsome gift was received.

'What! Do you say this fat child was born only yesterday? You women must be playing on our intelligence.' said Tamfu Bingir. At this rate, he should fetch water for me next month. You see, he is even able to hold something!' and he laughed.

'What a fat child!' Shei Ngabir exclaimed. 'Three days only and he is like this? Did he get strong in the womb before he was born? See him rolling his eyeballs from side to side. Please thank the mother very much for me. We thank Nyu for his marvelous gift'. He then pushed a coin into the tender hands which Ndapngong joyfully received on behalf of the baby.

The pride whelming up in Mama Njuh and Ma Ndabu could be seen even from a distance .It was overflowing. This time, when Mama Njuh sat with her pipe in hand, it was firmly gripped and the smoke rising from it was thick and gray-bright. She was either dishing out a rich laughter or entertaining her audience with fine jokes. The anxiety that had gripped her had rightly been replaced by true joy. 'You people,' referring to the Royal family, 'wanted to disgrace me. Who are you? I say who are you? Until my husband is dead you will never try me' she ended; and they all laughed.

In Nyamngong, the birth of a child especially the first born provided a mother -in-law the opportunity to boast and Mama Njuh had every reason to exploit it to the fullest. She herself knew that her daughter did not marry an offspring of a sheep but a lion, a fact for which she was proud and grateful. But that could not stop her from beating her chest. On the faces of Mama Njuh and Ma Ndabu were smiles of overwhelming joy. They were all victors and proud recipients of a bouncing healthy baby boy, Njemucharr, declared a special gift from Nyu Ngong.

Chapter Two

In his formative years, Njemucharr's growth was extraordinary. He bubbled with life. His fontanel had fully hardened when he was just half a year old. Instead of sitting and creeping for some time before walking; like every other human baby, Njemucharr one morning stunned all and sundry. Kwimnchep on failing to force him to sit down said: 'I will allow you to fall and that will teach you a lesson'. But as if to say 'Mami you will be surprised!' Instead of falling, he walked and that ended it. He was seven months and three days old then. Because of his rapid development and to avoid any uncontrollable behaviour on her part which may violate Ta Nwenchep's compelling instructions, Kwimnchep never carried him to other people's houses or compounds, especially to where there was any gathering. The child's size and weight was always her made-up excuse.

His conquest of language was so fast, and his ingenuity and creative power began unfolding quite early.

Nformi Birr would beam with satisfaction whenever he heard the boy asking highly intelligent questions or saw him trying to do things beyond the capabilities of a child of his age. Among his age mates and even those who were a bit older, he would assume the role of group leader due to his level of understanding. He loved sitting down and watching the father at work and would insist on helping him. Nformi Birr eager to watch the hidden talents in his child unfold with time exploited every given opportunity for good. He exploited the opportunity always offered by the boy's inquisitiveness. And being a man who never postponed a thing he never held back a thing on grounds that the child was too young except such that, in his judgment, was morally injurious.

'Papa what is that?' The son asked.

'It is a 'bie birr' (war shield)

'What are you doing with it?'

'I am dusting it. This sooth has made it look filthy.'

'What is it used for?'

'It is a weapon, indeed a shield, men who love their country protect themselves with it while at war with an enemy country which wants to kill them and take over their land or loot their property. You see, as a man, you should love people. But if somebody hates you and wants to make you a slave, hate him. Don't pretend and never give your head to somebody. You must love your country and be ready to defend and sacrifice for it. Your grandfather fought against the Whiteman and they killed him. He is a great man, respected with reverence all over Nyamngong and beyond, and people sing songs praising him. People talk about him proudly as if he were here with us today. For his good deeds, he lives in people's consciences. He is a hero.'

'Is Ta Nformi in?' greeted Tamfu, as he approached the door.

'Come right in, my brother,' Ta Nformi responded authoritatively.

Njemucharr greeted him respectfully, 'Welcome father!' as soon as he entered and dashed into the yard to join his playmates.

They exchanged greetings and asked about the health of every one in each family. Before they sat down to talk about the upcoming Nfu celebration in which HRH the Nyamndom was 'cleaning the floor of the Ndap Nfuh'; Tamfu remarked: 'I have realised that if it were in the days of the Bara mnya or tribal wars, Nyamngong would have produced an army general from the mother's breast', referring to Njemucharr. 'I could

14

not believe when I came in that you were discussing only with this kid. I expected a much grown up person.'

'Tamfu we just have to watch and see what type of man he shall be. He amazes me; his questions would keep you wondering if he were fed by someone else. May Nyu spare his life!' remarked his father beaming with joy; inwardly proud that Nyamngong dignitaries were already aware of the exceptional character of the boy, although he had never doubted the prediction. But like any ambitious father, he awaited the fulfillment anxiously. Nothing would be more satisfying and rewarding and nothing would give him a more peaceful death than the assurance that it was his own blood son to step into his shoes and perpetuate the great and respectable family name established by his father, Tatah Ngoh. 'In three generations of great men from the same family, never has such happened in history, he thought to himself. He peeped into the future and, seeing history being remade, congratulated himself 'But to make sure that nothing happens, I will do all I can. Is it not said that Nyu works wonders through human effort?' He confided to himself.

'Ta Nformi Birr, all of Nyamngong is alive and talking only of the coming Nfu celebration. The other day I was at the weekly market at Ndatamabebe and Gwei Nchoro was talking excitedly about it. He promised coming. It is going to be a real great day in the annals of our history' remarked Tamfu wiping the foam of palm wine from his thick mustache.

'True indeed' said Nformi Birr, refilling his cup. 'HRH the Nyamndom has so promised. The preparations are everywhere and no one is sleeping. As for Gwei Nchoro he can bring all of Ndatamabebe, there will be more than enough for them. I do not blame those who nicknamed him 'Yunka'. He should be prepared to sing, drum and compose new songs for this special occasion.' So they laughed with disgust at a title man whose best art is singing, drumming and dancing and who would never be absent at any funeral or celebration.

'Well if these are talents Nyu has blessed him with, who are we to…….'

'No, not that one is making a mockery or questioning. The point is that music is an art but he should not make a mockery of it and of himself. Why is he always the first to arrive and the last to leave a ceremony? Just watch, he shall be the first to arrive…'

'But you know it is through talented men like Gwei Nchoro that the young of tomorrow come to learn and know who we are and have been.'

'That is very true and that is why we wish that he should be here and compose new songs, create new dance styles and why not coin new titles for HRH the Nyamndom.'

'Without doubt, expect new things and even new terminologies that day and beyond.' Nformi Birr summed up as he refilled Tamfu's cup, then his.

They talked about many other things of interest to the community and this took them late into the evening when Tamfu took leave of his host.

'Thanks for the good palm wine and good kola nuts which I have some to take home and share with others. It has been an afternoon well spent with all the good discussions we have had. I know you will insist that I share your evening meal with you. After all this is a house of plenty. But I must go now' Tamfu said rising heavily from his chair.

'Yes there is goodness in sharing. Food tastes better when shared with one another. The more you share the more Nyu opens his doors for you. But I wonder how whites and big men enjoy their lives when they always live behind closed doors. But you must not behave like a white and leave on grounds that my wives did not include you in our evening meal. The

16

Nyamngong woman does not count mouths before cooking. I am sure the food is ready: my wives are not late night cooks

'But I must go and eat my own food so that it is not wasted. Thank you. Let me go' Tamfu, insisted.

'Good night then, if you insist. May Nyu let us see tomorrow!' said Ta Nformi Birr, as he stood up to lead his guest out of the house.

'Good night he who wrestles with the lions' Tamfu said as he slung his sheath machete and wore his title bag on the left arm to leave.

Chapter Three

It was a bright sunny afternoon. The compound was deserted except for the aged and the young ones. The men were either in the fields hunting, clearing new farms, or building huts in preparation for the planting season with the approaching, rainy season.

As for the women it was their busiest time. They had to till and mold the ridges of the old farms and the newly cleared farms. It is at moments like these when mothers identify suitable girls for their sons, and worthy sons-in-law are spotted out. Lazy ones, unable to bear the scorching inferno, sit to gossip under the tree shades. But this is not character of the Nyamngong woman or man. The stout structure of the Nyamngong is always associated with their devotion to hard work. At the end of a hard day's work, women return home in dust and ash because of heavy farm-work. The kids welcome their mothers with eagerness hoping to eat roasted cocoyam, cassava, yam or sweet potatoes brought from the farm. They taste better when one is really famished and has waited for them anxiously.

The intense sun sent Njemucharr and his age-mates to play under the kola nut trees. Being a regular playground it was clean of grass and dirt. They played all sort of games and were all exited. In all Njemucharr was either tuning the song or directing.

He was directing the game of' tiger and the goat '. At the height of it, Njemucharr screamed in pain 'ghaa...ah' as if stung by a scorpion and fainted to the ground. His fall to the ground followed by fits sent every play mate weeping and shouting for help. A couple of boys rushed to the compound

19

shouting 'Njemucharr is dead! 'Njemucharr is dead! Papa, come quickly!'

A serene noon was about to end in tragedy. The playground was invaded now by elders, each one carrying either his '*nsip mnchep*' or his medicine bag. Some cut fresh herbs mixed with either palm wine or water and forced his mouth open. With his nostrils closed tight the mixture was forced down his throat. Others using red palm-oil, mixed dried brown powdery medicine, and with the help of the forefinger forced the mixture into his mouth and forcing him to sniff some while the whole body was as well robbed with medicine mixed with palm oil.

Njemucharr behaved so mechanically. The tight teeth were no more rattling, but he groaned and bit his lips. The blue-eye bulbs were deeply buried into his head. The high fever was still on, despite the medication.

To avoid uncontrollable emotion, he was taken to his uncle's house. Kwimnchep, like all other women, unknowingly was busy in the farm. She was a hard working woman, producing every food crop known in Nyamngong.

In an effort to make fire for him, the uncle climbed into the ceiling for some dry wood. Leaning against the wall propped by others sitting by him, Njemucharr watched with all intensity as the uncle climbed on the ladder into the ceiling. As if being ushered into a different world, he saw fire burning down from the entrance into the ceiling. Tongues of fire of multiple darting colours of the most intense brightness lashed out, and he saw his uncle being engulfed in the flames. With all his might, he shouted 'Papa! Papa! Come down quickly. Jump down! The fire will burn you. Fire! Fire!!' Njemucharr pleaded earnestly with a fainting voice.

This stunned all who were in the house. The uncle shocked and confused asked, 'Where is the fire Njemucharr, my son?'

'See it descending from the ceiling,' he raised up the right hand weakly to demonstrate. It is already burning your head. Jump down Papa!' he shouted.

The uncle stood motionless with his hand still stretched into the ceiling, asked, 'My son, are you dying?'

'No Papa it is the fire. Please jump down. Fire! Fire!' and he dropped on the low bamboo bed as lightly as a bag of cotton

What transpired after this Njemucharr never knew. What brought him back to life was the thirst for water. His throat had gone as dry as hot coals. Though unconsciously, in the event of shouting for water from those beyond with whom he was struggling to communicate, he woke up to the relief of many. But to Kwimnchep he had mocked her and might depart. She wailed and pleaded with the gods to allow her Njemucharr. To her, taking Njemucharr was like taking the heart of a being and allowing the carcass.

After drinking the water so thirstily, as if, his life depended on it, he surveyed the house and was surprised to see many people weeping. He recognised the mother and bewildered, asked 'Mother, why are you crying?'

'I am crying because you want to go and leave me' she sobbed her answer.

Confused, Njemucharr asked, 'Where am I going, mother?'

'You are dying and I can't live without you.' she said trying to brighten up as men and women were urging her to stop weeping .Others speaking reassuringly, remarked he did not know what was happening and where he was.

As Njemucharr lay in bed, he tried to search his compact mind to know where he was. Failing to, he asked: 'Mother, where am I?'

'You are.........,' began one of his uncle's wives.

When it became obvious that Njemucharr's life hung in the balance he was taken to the great medicine man of the land, Tantoh Ncham Ncham. At dusk the women returned from their farms. On learning of what happened in the day, Kwimnchep was followed to the medicine man's residence by many for Njemucharr was a darling child to all and above all a child belongs to one person only when an unborn baby in the mother's womb.

The women heard Tantoh Ncham Ncham's voice and moved back mechanically. Others left, at least temporally. Every woman wiped her eyes and forced a bright face, for mourning does not take place near his residence or the shrine which stood immediately behind his house.

Round the house stood all kinds of plants and herbs, some of which you could never find anywhere else in the vicinity. Up in front of the house were tied bundles of bones of different animals, reptiles, feathers of every imaginable bird living, twigs, leaves, some which had long turned charcoal black due to the smoke that ushered its way out of the house every blessed second of the hour. It was said of him that his right hand had only one bone. For that reason, he never slapped someone with it, for the victim wouldl die instantly. As for his left arm, he never took it up, at least no one had ever seen him do so in public. Under the left armpit there were always three bones from the forelegs of a tiger.

It was said that inside his shrine he formed a rectangle with the bones to call up spirits and it was inside this rectangle that he threw his sorcery beads. And it was only under such circumstances that the bones could leave his armpit.

Being the toughest medicine man in living memory, people only consulted him in his home where he practised sorcery in his shrine. This island of a house was a world of its own; neither woman nor man had ever set foot inside.

'Who on earth brought all these women here to defile my medicine with their pots of tears? It was better you all left with your pots of water. If I see any eyelid wet, even Kwimnchep, you will have yourself to blame.' Tantoh Ncham Ncham threatened authoritatively not caring to look at the women or answer the many greetings from the visitors.

Kwimnchep was the first to speak out assuringly 'How can I weep when you are still living?' addressing him without taking up her face from the ground as a mark of respect. 'My concern was to bring the child to you, and now that he is here, I entertain no fear. Who in this land and beyond doubts Nyu-Ngong's hand through you in restoring life?'

As soon as Tantoh Ncham Ncham settled down in his shrine, he set to work to determine the source of the sickness. Recalling his prediction about Njemucharr, he told his admirers that the enemies were wasting their time. 'They are only hastening their own funeral oration and we have only one role to play, attend it. Not even a strand of hair can disappear from his head while I live' and he laughed, his toothless mouth agape, as he emphasised the 'I' beating his chest. The men joined him in the laughter to conceal their anxiety and eagerness to have him consult the spirits and tell them what to do to get the child up strong and healthy.

He shook his *Mbfuv seng* 'wuru, wuru, wuru' and poured the content on the leopard skin. This he did with exceptional regularity, precision and rhythm. On the third count he burst out laughing, 'Ha! , Ha! Ha! See them. Naked woman and spineless man! Has a monkey ever succeeded in hiding its ugly face with its palms? And he laughed so heartily again.

All those who heard him understood nothing. It was as if Tantoh Ncham Ncham had set their anxiety on the sharp edge of razor blade. But Tantoh Ncham Ncham being who he was, took his time. He had his own music and you had no choice but to dance to the rhythm of his music. A master of his own arts, once before him, you have no choice. You can't make him act faster or talk when he does not want to. 'Only Nyu Ngong controls and dictates to me, no mortal being,' he would say proudly.

'Tantoh why all this? What do you want us to see? Would we have been here if we could see or if we could communicate with the spirit world?! Nyu knows why he gives to others and ....' Queried Pa Ngibuh, leader of the team sent to find out the cause of the illness.

'Yes I know' Tantoh Ncham Ncham, in the manner of men with double eyes cut in proudly completing the statement, 'and deny others.' It is a pity!' He held out an old black bead. 'This is the old woman, the witch. And here is the man.' He pushed aside the sharp edge of the spear, 'who, with this old woman, are responsible for this boy's sickness.' The two objects were pushed far apart from all the rest.

'They are not trying to kill him. They can't. They want to mislead him from our Creator's already charted path into their evil ways, pollute his mind, poison his consciousness, and distort his perception so that, at the end, he would fail in his mission. With this achieved, their own kind will take over. No wonder a wizard is called *'Nwe- tfu'* in *Lingong*,. There could never have been a most fitting name than this.' He laughed until tears ran down his old brown eyes.

Tantoh Ncham Ncham's sharp eyes which bellied their frailty when fixed on you, could charge like an electric circuit. When performing his magic, no one dared look at him straight in the eyes. Lips and fingers move. Under such circumstances, he was in communication with the invincible powers, the source of his own might.

24

The *'mbfu seng'* an old gourd neatly shaped from the region the neck begins to thin out. It was indeed a cave of its own. From it poured a rusty curie, mark, a penny, beads of different kinds and sizes, the tooth of a dog, the head of a lizard, the tooth of a lion, a piece of raffia palm nut, the end of a quill, the end of a spear, a piece of cloth, some three round pebbles, some small hair, a small piece of glass. There were of all colours and shapes. Being a messenger of Nyu-Ngong, the supreme God, no mortal being could have mastered the art of creating **mbfu seng** and its perplexing content but the Creator himself who assembled them and handed the **mbfu seng** to Tantoh Ncham Ncham to serve mankind.

A medicine man has never exhibited such confidence and originality over his art. Sorcery to Tantoh Ncham Ncham was both art and science from the Supreme Being in which truth, service, honesty and fidelity were watch words. As he poured out his lot, he chanted the required incantations, he conversed aloud, queried invisible beings, quarrelled and stunned those around him as he grinned and laughed to himself. Before he gathered the whole, a thing which he did in three scoops, he spat gently unto the lot three times grinding what remained of his once full mouth. As soon as he discovered the cause, he gathered the lot back and covered the feather bowl with the leopard skin. No pressure could persuade him to uncover it once covered and to do any sorcery again. 'I have handed over. I can't go back to them now,' he would adamantly insist.

Until the cause of the sickness was known he never gave any medicine to the sick. But if on the other hand the spirits informed him that the soul was already in the world beyond or in the hands of **Nkwiyir** (Death) or had gone to **Mbanyir**, he received no consultation kola and palm-wine that was brought. If the patient had been brought, the relations would be advised to take him back immediately. He argued that his house represented life, and this was the force of the healing powers of his medicine.

After his recovery Njemucharr revealed to his playmates what he saw during his transfiguration. Njemucharr who had always been a puzzle and an enigmatic character, not only to his play-mates but also to elders, created sensation to some and terrified others.

'The first thing that happened to me was the prompt disappearance of pain. The hard bamboo bed which I had lain on suddenly became layers of cushion, and I found myself descending softly as if to land; but this never happened.

'The world into which I descended was extra-ordinarily peaceful, cool, refreshing, luxuriant, rich to the extent that I felt the richness and beauty in me. The paths were perfectly bright, made of fine marble and gold. The air that I inhaled was pure. Evidence of wealth and abundance needed no word. Maximum comfort for everyone was certainly the governing principle. In my descending flying mode, though wingless, my legs folded below, I saw from a height a perfectly straight path, and apparently broad running as far as the eye could see. On both sides were flowers of different colours and attracting sweet scent .The flowers were perfectly kept with lawns on both sides of the inviting express-way. At the far end of it were many men sitting in a circle in exceptionally dazzling white garments. Moving towards them was an elder Ya-ah Ma Nye (Queen) in her regalia and smoking a long pipe adorned in symbols of royalty.

'In all my efforts', Njemucharr emphasised, 'I tried to attract attention to no avail. I called on the Ya-ah Ma Nye, whom I recognised and identified as such just from her regalia, Mama! Mama! Mama! But, to my disappointment, she continued her graceful march towards those sitting in a circle in gorgeous white garments. I tried with all my strength to race towards her and the group seated further, but my feet could take me nowhere. My shouting to attract their attention fell short of kindling their sympathy. None as much as turned to look at me. It may be it was my shouting and struggling to run that made me too thirsty!' He concluded to the admiration and shock of his colleagues who were so tongue tied that not even one of the so many questions in their minds could be pronounced. It was as if a rat was dead in their mouths.

Chapter Four

Whenever the school came to the Royal Palace, Nyamntoh, for an occasion, Njemucharr would take his insect-hunting bag to follow them. He was always thrilled by their orderly marching, their neatness and the ability of those who could read and speak the white-man's language. At one time, when the school came with fire-wood to give to HRH the Nyamndom, Njemucharr cried to follow them, and the head-teacher had to intervene. When he heard why the kid was crying, he was glad that their effort to attract princes and princesses to school had started to yield fruit. It was in those days when schooling was seen as a thing for commoners, when princes and princesses occupied enviable traditional positions and enjoyed high privileges. It was a serious crime to beat a prince or princess, so they were contented with their traditional privileges and roles. They could not be sent to school and be defiled by the hand or cane meant for commoners.

To console him, the Head-teacher took his right hand and put it over his head asking him to touch his left ear with his index finger. Since he could not touch it very well he was told to wait a bit for next school session. He was only comforted with the promise that he would be big for school the coming year.

Njemucharr greatly admired Ringnda's ability to understand the Whiteman who spoke from his nostrils. Ringnda, a young brilliant boy, was the first from the nearby village to enter Empire Provincial College, the first post primary institution in the province. In addition to academic brilliance, he was a fast runner and footballer. During the Empire Day Celebration which took place once a year, he won a lot of prices, books, blankets, buckets, cutlasses and money. These were treasures not available in many homes in those days, but Ringnda's parents had them in abundance. Indeed they never used calabashes in fetching water, nor did his father eat from calabash bowls and clay pots any longer.

Ringnda had also visited other big towns in the territory to participate in inter-provincial matches and sports. He was well known and admired for bringing honour and sun shine into his home.

All these made him so popular and well loved by both students and teachers. He was also loved by the missionaries, for he was quite active in the local church. Back home, he was admired and respected by the young ones. His parents themselves prided in him and talked of him as the ruler of the field. The young women would respectfully address his mother as 'mother of the swift feet'.

Njemucharr never forgot the promise of the Head teacher. He looked up to next year with the eagerness of an ardent Moslem who looks for the face of the moon to enable him break his fast and feast. Although he did not know how long he would have to wait, he expected the next year, to mature in the nearest future .As he looked forward to next year he was not oblivious of the fact that it was his inability to cross his right hand over his head and touch his left ear that postponed his going to school. To make sure that there was again no postponement he made enough practice. He would tilt the head and on holding the ear would call out 'Mama! Mama! I have touched it very well; can I go tomorrow?'

'How can you go tomorrow whereas the head -teacher said next year?' Kwimnchep would say convincingly admiring the resourcefulness of her son.

'But I am big. No need waiting. I want to be like Ringnda so that you would be a proud mother and all other women would admire and respect you'.

'You are not even touching your ear very well. In school they read and write. They don't spend time eating and playing. Hunger will kill you there." Kwimnchep would tease her beloved son.

'Mama I will not die,' Njemucharr would say skipping around and beaming with smiles. He continued persisting until the day he went to school.

In class- work he proved an intelligent chap. As regards outdoor activities such as sports, he did not excel. He loved games and while in the senior primary, he was in the school football team.

His teachers loved him dearly for he was witty, creative, intelligent, obedient and respectful. His family background placed him above all others and despite his wealth and all other facilities that set him apart, he was never proud or arrogant. He was a dandy lad of the first class and was always so conscious of what he wore. His academic brilliance, his neatness and handsomeness matched with his skin's fair complexion made him the centre of attraction.

As for the girls, it was a great pride to be associated with Njemucharr. He was always ready to help the low in intelligence understand the lessons and solve their problems. As for his generosity there was no limit. He was a friend to all and a foe to none.

At the end of his primary school career, Njemucharr scored the highest marks in the First School Leaving Certificate (FSLC) examination in the Province .The Head teacher and the entire staff was highly gratified and they planned for a special end of year Parent Teachers Association (PTA) get together to celebrate this memorable achievement which brought great honour to the school for the first time in the history of the province.

The surrounding villages were all gratified with the news that it was going to be a great day, and that many important people were going to attend. HRH the Nyamndom was invited as a special guest of honour. It was always a throng whenever HRH was to feature in any occasion. Unlike any other PTA to mark the end of year, a lot of activities were going to feature amongst which were sports competitions, traditional dances, recitations by the best pupils of each class, among others.

On the PTA Honourary Day, as it came to be called respectfully, fathers, mothers, relations and well-wishers streamed into the school from far and near. More than ever before, they contributed so generously that the ever efficient and meticulous Mr. Wepnje lost count of the calabashes of palm wine, baskets of corn- flour, pods or tied bundles of kola nuts, and even fowls. HRH the Nyamndom sent eight calabashes of palm wine and a huge castrated he- goat. Mr. Wepnje had a real tough task making sure that everyone was well- fed not because there was scarcity but because there were many people. With exceptional planning and organization, everyone drank and ate to his fill and left satisfied.

Then came the climax of the celebration. The Head teacher after thanking HRH the Nyamndom and all for honouring their invitation and for their generous contributions, he elatedly expressed the honour Njemucharr won for the school. 'Since the creation of the centralized examination system fifteen years ago, only the provincial capital schools had been winning and keeping the trophy. But today our own son, Njemucharr, has proven to us that the white- man and children of big men do not have superior intelligence as we are made to believe' he said.

To enable his audience get the true picture, he explained to them that the provincial capital school were special schools, built and better equipped for the children of the whites who were ruling, the merchants and the missionaries. The only black children were those of the few black men in big positions, who had forgotten their mother tongue, our traditions and customs, and who tried to behave and live like the white man.

There was evidence of surprise, hissing laughter from the audience and some expressed pity for lost souls and the self-outcast.

Throughout the merry-making, Njemucharr was the real centre of attraction. Many parents greeted him, congratulating him with an affectionate firm hand- shake. Others gave him presents. Some, in admiration, cross-examined his handsome sunny-broad face as if to see the amount of intelligence that put him above the white man's child.

The Award- giving ceremony which was the high mark of the occasion was under the distinguished patronage of Hon Bongbih, (MP) whom the Head teacher described as a true nationalist, a man for his people and fighter for natural justice, human freedom and dignity.

'I thank the Head-teacher and his lieutenants for inviting me and according me such great honour. To His Royal Highness the Nyamndom, his able Counselors, nobles, our elders and all, I thank you all for making this day a great day in the history of this school. 'You have made many good remarks about me, how as an MP I have been in the forefront of our National party fighting for our independence. Thanks for the good remarks and the promise to continue to support the struggle for national liberation and true independence. From your speech, I believe you are training these young ones to be truly disciplined nationalist leaders of our fatherland. The future of this great country lies in our hands. We must distinguish ourselves in selflessly fighting to bequeath a rich legacy to our descendants. We must pave the way for a bright future in freedom and prosperity. This country belongs to us and not the strangers who have imposed themselves over us because of skin pigmentation. For us to bequeath a befitting legacy to our descendants we must work hard to be masters of our destiny.

'You have also made good comments about your pupil, Njemucharr, whose name is now written in the annals of our history as the first black child to score the highest mark in the province, thus proving that he is more intelligent than the white man's children and the children of the black- white men. The capital school was built for superior pupils. This is what we are fighting against: racism, nepotism, segregation and deprivation. This country is our own and we should either all enjoy or all suffer. And not that some should enjoy at the expense of others'.

This was received with a prolonged applause. Behind him, HRH the Nyamndom nodded his royal head approvingly. Minutes passed by before silence was restored, as there were comments of general approval from the audience.

People have always loved to listen to Hon. Bongbih. Each time he spoke he gave to the people what they wanted to hear. It was always as if he read people's minds before addressing them. This explains why he was called the People's Leader.

'Njemucharr', he picked on, 'our son went to war against the white- man, the so- called superior people and defeated them. This was the war of the pen, paper and brain. The pen and paper were brought to us by the white man and if a child of our own loins should use this instrument and defeat the white- man, then this is double victory. Firstly, the belief that the white- man is invulnerable is a myth. Secondly, it is a pointer that greater victory would surely be achieved if we resolutely, determinedly and solidly stand by one another and commit ourselves to the ultimate goal, namely, freedom and independence.

At the linking of Njemucharr's victory with those of his grandfather Tatah Ngoh, whose military prowess and magical powers earned him the name 'red leopard' there was prolonged applause and jubilation. Someone from the crowd, overwhelmed with the logic of the analogy, screamed, 'the voice that declares the will of the people, is the voice of God'

In the prize award ceremony, Njemucharr received four of the seven prizes the highest being that in recognition of his able leadership as the school senior head- boy.

The Provincial Academic Prize (PAP) was the last to be announced. As the name Njemucharr Nformi Birr was called out, it was greeted with thunderous applause. His father overwhelmed with joy, stood from amongst the crowd and sang a war- song, taking some athletic moves of triumph.

Njemucharr received the prestigious Prize Award. It was a gold medal which Hon. Bongbih hung on his neck. He handed him a Certificate, after brandishing it before the public, and an envelope containing the cash award, the amount which was not announced to the anxious audience. He shook Njemucharr's hand vigorously and embraced him warmly to the great admiration of all.

As soon as Njemucharr stepped down, he moved straight to his father and handed him the sealed envelope and the gold medal. This act did his father great pride and honour in the eyes of his admirers. In Nyamngong it was expected of any obedient and well-brought up child never to receive any gift for personal use, but rather to surrender it completely to the parents. It was for the parents to decide what to do with the gift.

Back home, there was great rejoicing. Relations beat their chest in their weekly Mndap ngwa, in the weekly market places, and everywhere they found cause for boasting, having produced an embodiment of super intelligence. Others called Njemucharr 'bfih gha nkfu'or 'sense pass king'

As for presents, they were many and varied; coins mostly from men, groundnuts, tadpoles on strings from young girls and mothers. According to Nyamngong tradition, every woman in the family had maternal obligations to every child. The Nyamngong culture and tradition could nowhere be pursued to the letter and spirit than in Nyamntoh, the royal family which served as the custodian and sanctuary. Njemucharr's good character coupled with his handsome build earned him a good place in the heart of every one. This occasion at school provided a unique opportunity where such obligations were manifested and the gifts that poured in proved this.

His parents killed a big cock for him and gave him a live hen. The killing of the cock demonstrated the importance the parents attached to what Njemucharr had done through the pen. Under normal circumstances, a chicken was slaughtered for celebration, as sacrifices for cleansing, or for the entertainment of an important in- law. The roasting of a chicken for a visitor is a mark of great honour for him or her and it is mandatory that the visitor takes home part of the chicken as evidence of the red carpet treatment received. Here Njemucharr was just greatly elevated by his parents. He had carved for himself a name in the annals of history of Nyamngong and provided material for new composition by the damsels and musicians of the land and the songs came in, in their numbers.

Tar Mangong, The Nyamndom, presented him with a spotless, black goat, except for the white star on its forehead.

The goat was already pregnant. Njemucharr received this special present with reverence, and thanked His Royal Highness heartily. He solemnly promised to shine and uplift the good and enviable name of the family. With these manly and consciously pronounced words, HRH the Nyamndom made his libations three times, rubbed his right forefinger on the spot three times and with that finger made a straight line on his forehead. This was a blessing even though Njemucharr did not understand its meaning and significance. The nobles, who were always with HRH the Nyamndom right in the inner chambers, curbed their hands, clapped three times and with their hands lifted to their mouths greeted: 'bfuruh' (the lion). They totally understood the extent of the blessing.

Chapter Five

It was unexpected. But as tradition demanded, once Tar-Mangong, HRH the Nyamndom convoked his subjects, all gathered enthusiastically in the Court Yard of the People. He never convoked his people for his personal pleasure; it was always in the supreme interest of the people and the land.

HRH called on Ta Shey Ntoh to place two objects in the centre of the Court Yard. These objects were a 'calabash' and a 'bottle of beer,' both empty.

From the Royal Throne came brisk instructions to all those assembled: 'Examine the two objects very well.'

From a distance, all eyes, male and female, young and old were fixed on the two objects, 'the bottle' and 'the calabash'. Certainly every searching eye must have been out scanning the objects to see if at all there was anything extraordinary.

Njemucharr and his colleagues, who were on holidays, were equally keen. But both the bottle and the calabash were familiar objects. To Njemucharr the only difference his fertile inquisitive mind could deduce was that while the calabashes were produced in Nyamngong and other kingdoms for various purposes, the bottle was introduced into the land by the white man through the importation of beer and other finished products. And this was an ordinary beer bottle, a '33 Export empty bottle.

When HRH, Tar Mangong was satisfied that his subjects had had enough time to studiously examine the two objects, he heaved the Royal cough, 'Kbu-hu.' With this the nobles and titled- men curbed their hands and greeted '*Tfub! Tfub! Tfub!' 'bfuruf!'* And every one adjusted himself expectantly.

'My people, tell me,' called HRH, Tar Mangong, 'Of these two objects, which is older?'

The whole Court Yard of the People went perfectly dead. Not even a whisper and not even a baby cried. Nature itself stood still except for a gentle breeze. Even the birds that had been singing in the kola nut trees stopped. Were they searching for an answer too or were they, like HRH the Tar Mangong, waiting for an answer from the subjects? It was as if even the suckling strapped on their mothers' backs were equally searching for an answer or waiting for. Every mind and nerve was stretched to breaking point, painstakingly doing one thing or the other in relation to HRH's puzzle.

Njemucharr on his part did not know if he should apply his small knowledge of history with its dates to determine when an event or an act took place to answer or whether he should apply his small knowledge of biology. None seemed to suit the situation. He concluded that the Tar Mangong had put out a puzzle which had no answer. This conclusion notwithstanding, his admiration for HRH only increased. Then he recalled cheerfully that HRH while blessing him called on him 'to shine like the sun and the moon'. His own very ears heard his heart beat throbbing, as if he had gone through an awful nightmare. He took up his eyes and saw that every head was still bowed.

Soon Fai Ndi Mbeh gave a throaty cough and moved forward, curbed his hands and greeted, '*Bfu'ruf*'

HRH, the Tar Mangong acknowledged with a royal node.

'Your Highness, may your reign be long and prosperous. May the Omnipotent and Omniscient Nyu Ngong be gracious and endow you with wisdom for the greatness of this kingdom,' and he adjusted his flowing robes.

'*Bfu'ruf,* as to your question which has stretched the nerves of every mind to breaking point; may I use my old brains to attempt an answer. The calabash is older than the bottle.'

And he curbed his hands and greeted, '*Bfu'ruf*' before resuming his position among the nobles.

To the people who heard the answer given by Fai Ndi Mbeh, there was still a question mark. Only the confirmation by HRH Tar Mangong would convince anxious minds, or take confused minds to another planet of wonderland.

It was a big relief, even to Njemucharr and his college mates, when Tar Mangong said, 'Fai Ndi Mbeh, you have spoken well.

'But what do the two objects represent? Are they related? Do they and can they perform the same function in our land?' HRH set every mind once again afield.

'Now my people listen attentively. The calabash represents our time honoured tradition, customs and culture. Indeed that which distinguishes a Nyamngong and makes him distinct from peoples of other worlds. You are not only a Nyamngong because you speak Lingong. You are not only a Nyamngong because you were born here and your navel buried on the land of our ancestors. All these are important ingredients. But what makes you distinct, and that, which you must be proud of, is the Nyamngong tradition, custom and culture which has nourished you, built you up, and endowed you with a consciousness that makes you different. It gives you your own personality and belief about the here and the hereafter, the visible and the invisible world, your likes and your hates.

'It is in defense of this self-consciousness, self-worth and core cultural values that you exhibit your inherent identity, dignity and equality with other peoples of other lands. Your culture is your identity card; it makes you distinct and equal to other peoples. As you are different from other people, so are others different from you. Your being different from other people of other lands does not make you inferior or deficient. But you make yourself inferior by abandoning your cultural values and trying to make yourself a photocopy of other people. To be a copy cat of foreign cultures is to betray your inherent identity, worth, dignity. This leads you to lose the centre of your balance, that is, the natural umbilical cord with your ancestors, land and history.

'No culture is static. Every culture is dynamic and grows through human positive activity. But to slavishly copy foreign cultures you dislocate your inherent potential for development. By this treacherous act you declare yourself inferior and make yourself a slave of the people you believe are superior to you.' And he gave a long breath to enable what has been said to sink in.

But as every mind was in solemn reflection, all knew HRH was yet to land. It was a rare moment and the Tar Mangong, the custodian of the culture and land of the people and the embodiment of the people's will, has a unique way of passing judgement and issuing edicts.

'The calabash,' HRH picked on, 'represents our time honoured cultural values, our land, and our heritage. The calabash is a product of our effort. The way it is designed, the artistic decorations and fortifications illustrates our love of beauty and originality. The calabash is us. But what does the bottle represent? It represents foreign values, strange customs, maddening some among you,' and he furiously thrust the royal hand. The thrusting was so vehement that HRH jerked forward as if rising on his feet. This would have been out of the nature of things, for Royal proclamations were made from the throne, the symbol of authority. Authority is in the institution, the incarnation of the people's will and not in the individual.

'That bottle, as small as it is, its content is poisonous. It is turning our culture and traditions upside down. Its content is cancerous, it's a virus that destroys the fabrics of the cultural heart of our people. Respect for the elders, our traditions and customs and cultural values are heavily being eroded by this invader, the beer; the victim is not the individual, it is the people, their cultural values, their ancestral land and the respect and honour which we as a people enjoy from others when we in all our acts, character and attitude demonstrate that we are proud to be Nyamngong and will exchange this identity with no other. That is living honourably, living the Nyamngong way. You must defend and project what being a Nyamngong means to you. You must hate doing anything that brings dishonor to your being, your family and your country Nyamngong in general.

'It is sad, really sad and dishonourable to see what is happening in our land.' This statement of lamentation caught the attention of every one gathered as HRH said this shaking the royal head sadly. This was out of the ordinary. No one had heard of grave development in the land. This statement however only generated keen interest and all glued to the Throne to hear what had happened or was amiss.

'Today,' HRH picked up on a louder note; 'mothers in the markets, in bars have forgotten their roles. Just because of that stranger,' he pointed at the bottle, 'I mean a bottle of beer, and mothers give out their daughters in marriage without the knowledge of their husbands and the family. It is same for our daughters, who single-handedly negotiate their marriage without the consent of the family. You are not an island. You are part and parcel of your family and Nyamngong in general. Our elders say that because the Mbei River travelled alone it could not go straight; it had to wind and wind making so many bends in its cause.

'This is in total violation of our time-honoured traditions. Yes I banned the ancient practice of forcing girls into marriage against their will. But this is not a license for waywardness. Marriage is not an individual affair. With our palm-wine in the calabash, the two families concerned and friends are united, and unity through blood relationship is eternal. Marriages have consolidated the unity of Nyamngong. It is the unity of families, eternal bonds of friendship, the belief in oneness, the sense of belonging that builds communal spirit, the eternal sharing of love in joy and sharing or showing concern in sadness, feeling and caring for one another, among others; all this accounts for stability in marriage. Divorce is unknown in our land; a man needs a woman and vice versa, marriages make us share both in joy and sadness, abundance and scarcity. This is what Nyu Ngong instituted marriage to be. Our sense of being one another's keeper and having a deep sense of belonging has from the beginning of times, grown from strength to strength and marriage is the foundation. Harmony in the conduct of marriage works for stability in marriage and family stability does not only account for unity and prosperity of the family, the clan, it works for the greatness of Nyamngong in general. When people outside talk well of the good character of the Nyamngong woman, they revere Nyamngong.

'These bonds of oneness and unity are being shattered by this poisonous intruder, the beer, which has introduced a virus, individualism, self-centredness. This is only one area of corruption that bottle has introduced into our land. Drunkenness, addiction to alcohol, love of beer as a kind of manifestation of new social status attained, which brings with it many social evils such as disrespect, waywardness is on the rise; alarming rise,' his voice sounded hoarse.

'That bottle will encourage licentiousness. It will kill the spirit of industry. Addiction to alcohol and beer cannot stimulate productivity. Our women used to drink only sweet palm wine. But today some are indulging into drinking beer and spirits, even refusing to drink soft drinks such as Sprite, Orange, amongst others, claiming that it makes them vomit. Women are now coming back home from market late at night. This is not in the nature of a Nyamngong woman, the staying force of our rich cultural heritage. The women are not only the mothers of the Nyamngong dynamic youths of tomorrow; they constitute the main-stay of our culture and progressive Nyamngong.

'This beer is importing and imposing strange cultural values, corrupting the minds of the youths, the women and even some spineless men and titled elders. The fabrics of our cultural cohesion are being destroyed by this bottle which is imposing a new religion and false identity. Individualism and self-interest are replacing collective consciousness and communal spirit. This will flood our land with evil and crimes unheard-of. Once self-interest replaces collective interest, greed replaces communal spirit, and foreign values replace our time-honoured cultural values; treachery will find its way into our land.

'We must check and control this with every iota of strength and faith in our self-worth and keep this evil beyond our territorial frontiers.

'No agreement, traditional and other- wise, should be entered into by any Nyamngong on a bottle of beer. All agreements must be sealed in honour, fidelity on a calabash of palm wine and the traditional kola.

'No agreement should be concluded with whomever to protect self-interest. Every agreement must be reached and concluded in the presence of other Nyamngong nobles and people. No one, man or woman, should act in any manner to bring dishonour to our land. Our land must remain the eternal heritage of our people, posterity, the ancestors and the gods and we the rulers, the custodians,' HRH concluded.

While he spoke people stood speechless and motionless. Not even a baby cried. As if to say nature honoured him, the noon- day hot sun had disappeared behind a thick layer of clouds. This created an enviable atmosphere for such a proclamation. It was a proclamation for the ages and the future.

'Fai Ndingah Nwenfu, where are you? Move to the centre. Fai Ndi Dodoh, join him. Put the wood ash on the spot,' and he did respectfully, curbed his hands and greeted, 'Nyui' as he always did.

It was the turn of Fai Ndingah Nwenfu, the second in command. He adjusted his traditional flowing gown, moved towards the throne and greeted, 'Bfu'ruf'! Tar Mangong! Your voice is the voice of Nyu Ngong!'

He then moved to the centre spot, the usual spot for such a solemn act, oath- taking.

'As the Throne has spoken, we all here assembled will have to take an oath before the Throne, our ancestors and Nyu Ngong. Man, woman and child of Nyamngong will take the oath.

'We are taking this oath to;

-Reaffirm our loyalty to the Throne

-Reaffirm our abiding faith in our cultural values

-Declare our commitment to uphold, preserve, protect, defend and promote our inherent identity.

-Uncompromisingly reject foreign corrupt values being imported into our land.

-Pledge never to betray one another, and our land, and to defend and protect our land at all times, come what may. '

After making known the principles on which the oath was being taken, he gave room for each, beginning with the notables, title holders, the men, the women and the young ones, each to take a pinch of the wood ash. One after the other all filed in solemnly and scooped the wood ash.

Fai Ndingah Nwenfu, seeing that the stage was set for the final act, with his own quantity of wood ash in hand, he then resumed his role.

'Mbalee!' Fai Ndingah Nwefu rented the air with his heavy masculine voice.

'Bong abee!' the crowd answered enthusiastically.

'Mbalee!' he called out again.

'Bong abee!' the crowd answered.

'Mbalee! He called the third time.

'Abee yu ngir' and they answered in unison.

'Mbalee, should an individual betray the people, should one go against the will of the people, should he perish alone or the people?'

'He is the one to perish with his sins and not the people,' the people chanted their answer.

'Should someone betray the people and the land, who should perish?'

'The gods of the land should strike him instantly dead with his intestines exposed and bless the people to live and prosper,' the people in unison chorused their answer.

He asked again the third time and all unanimously answered same.

On this third count all blow the wood-ash into the air, shouting *'Yo bee-bee o!' Yo bee-bee o!!' 'Yo bee-bee o!!!' 'Let the evil go with the evil doer! Let the evil go with the evil doer!! Let the evil go with the evil doer!!!'*

Tar Mangong, thanked them all and majestically rose from the Throne to retire into the Inner Chambers of the Palace.

His satisfaction was greeted enthusiastically by the notables and titled men.

It was with his departure that the people's spirits loosened and their eyes opened. They then exchanged greetings with one another. Within the two and half hours conclave they were held spell- bound and focused on the Throne and anxious to know what was at stake.

Their anxieties had been kindled; expectations heightened and Tar Mangong, HRH the Nyamndom had poured out his love for his people, the land and the future. As they retired home, all confessed that the gods had made some great strategic revelations to them against imminent evil over the land if they should allow strange ideas and, culture in the name of fashion.

As HRH the Nyamndom had warned most emphatically, 'Change should not come to our land through deceit and treachery, it should not be brought in by the whirl- wind through the window. Any change forced on us, is not for our good. Change must germinate and grow from within, and the Nyamngong must be the master and agent of change. Change must be the fruit of the people's positive action. And this change must be for the good of all and the land. Change to be positive must sustain growth and development and promote justice and happiness.'

Njemucharr left, wondering aloud whether the belief his people hold that the word of HRH the Nyamndom is the word of the gods is true. 'It should be true,' he concluded. 'If not, how could a mortal being use a calabash and a beer bottle to make such a great pronouncement full of wisdom?' he reflected keenly in admiration. Happily he thanked his stars for having been on holidays to live such an experience he will live to remember

Chapter Six

'Ma Bowa, I have invited you and our dear son for a purpose. Our son is bubbling with good health and is growing very fast. He is now in college. We thank Nyu Ngong for the blessings. I want us to reflect on what transpired in the Palace yesterday. We were all there. We saw and we heard what HRH said to his people about their heritage, destiny and their country.'

'Yes Tar Bo, since we got married, I have attended many such gatherings at the Court Yard of the People. But that of yesterday was unique. What was spectacular and baffled me was not only the huge turnout; it was what HRH said about some women indulging into consumption of beer and even spirits. It made me shudder at what is becoming of our womanhood in the senselessness of modernity.'

'Is it HRH the Nyamndom saying it? Have you not seen?'

'Yes Tar Bo, I have seen. But the most disturbing thing is what was said that mothers are beginning to give their daughters in marriage in the markets on a bottle of beer. Eh my Mami,' she exclaimed clapping her hands in disgust. 'That what? Wonders shall never end.'

'Is that all you heard? I know you are a very clever woman.'

'Well Tar Bo, what do you want me to say as if you corked your ears with bee wax. He also said that some women due to excessive alcohol consumption become obstinate and misbehave.'

'Thank you. The issue at stake was not just about women. The declaration was made to all of us, fathers, mothers, children and even the future generation. That gathering of yesterday and the declaration made will be remembered for ages. It is a timeless declaration. It will stand in testimony for or against some among us. It is for this reason I invited you for profound reflection. The family is the foundation of the nation. Any man who fails to put order, discipline in his house properly and responsibly cannot be a good leader of the community or nation. The rotten eggs of the nation are the bad eggs of respective families. To work for a strong, united and prosperous nation we must build strong families where love, obedience, honesty, justice, discipline, hard work and respect are cardinal.

'Being responsible, sensitive to the feelings of others, being honest, being just and promoting social justice in society and being duty conscious are strong qualities of a good man who cares and works for the growth and development of his society and country and the family remains the foundation. It is small good acts that we do that positively impact the lives of others. Good character and a good deed to one person have a multiplier effect. Greet someone with a smile and he will open up. Come into a room with a sunny face and you will light the house and bring in hope and cheerfulness to all. These qualities must be inculcated in our children from infancy.

'Why from infancy you may ask? As a farmer if you want your yams to bear heavily you must stake early in the season and let the stems climb. Know that when the mother mouse is climbing the walls of the house the kitten (baby) is down watching keenly. This requires that the mother must do what it has to do rightly and purposefully. This is the training which is required for proper upbringing and development of the human person.

'The role of parents is critical in the nurturing of good children. Knowing what is good is a step in the right direction. But living according to the tenets of what is good and upright and impacts the lives of others is living a fulfilled life as ordained by Nyu Ngong the Creator of the universe and humankind who has the power to make and unmake.

'Some children ignorantly complain of their parents and some grown up people complain of their village where they were born and would compare with other people's village or town. Such talk as if they have the power to exchange so that they could be happy somewhere else or with the so-called good parents they admire. That is silly idle thoughts. Why complain of what you can't change my son?' and he laughed so scornfully. 'You try to be someone else, you ridicule yourself. You cannot be a king in someone's house. But the Creator has made you a king in your own house, your own village and your own country.

'But father, is it wrong to admire what someone has which you don't have?'

'That is a good question my son. Look at the fingers on your hand. Are they the same? Firstly accept what you have and be proud of who you are. Nyu Ngong created each person and each people unique. No one is a photocopy of the other nor can you change yourself to be the other person. This is what HRH was emphasising yesterday. Why do we learn? Why have I been talking of hard work and duty consciousness? We work to improve our condition of life. My father's house was smaller than this that I have built. When I was a kid the palace you see today did not have the large court yard and magnificent carvings, decorations and structures you have today. And I believe when your generation grows up, you shall carry on further improvements and development by putting up magnificent buildings.

'Why did Nyu Ngong so graciously and generously give you hands, feet, eyes, ears and intelligence? Look at our country, Nyamngong and Fakulum! You think if the white man had all these good things that we have he would have come

51

here? I hear in their country sometimes it is too cold and for many weeks they do not even have sun shine and the poor and old people die in their beds. If we use our hands and the knowledge Nyu Ngong has given us we will develop our country. Through hard work, duty consciousness and love of our country we will transform our country and live happily.

'There can be no nationalist, no patriot who as a child was not an obedient child, was not a strong lover and respecter of his parents and who did not grow up to adore and believe in his family, seeing the family as unique and a strong fortress, who did not love his village, ethnic community. As one grows in his village and dreams of transforming his village so will he be a nationalist and patriot and work to defend and promote the good image of his nation in which lies his small village or ethnic community. The nationalist and patriot must firmly believe in the unity of all the ethnic communities within the territorial boundaries to build a strong united and progressive nation serving the interests of all its citizens equally.

'Ma Bo, I see you are so mindful about what HRH said about the negative changing attitude and habits of some women. From the declaration of HRH The Nyamndom you may say 'I don't yet have a daughter, so I am not affected.' No! You are. What concerns the Nyamngong womanhood concerns you. What concerns Nyamngong identity and culture concerns us all. Your memory of how your dear mother used to teach you how to behave, good manners of a girl, how to take care of your junior brothers, how to till the farm, make mounts for yams, cook and dish food making sure that everyone, even the visitor who could come, had a fair share, is not dead and forgotten. That is why our house is always warm for visitors. In Nyamngong every girl is a prospective wife of some boy and every boy a prospective husband of some girl, and respectively to be a mother or a father with clear roles and mission. Such training from birth, I should say, for responsibility, sensitivity, caring, being one another's brother, showing love and respect, and great emphasis on defence of truth, on honesty, service to the community, obedience and discipline, is part of the upbringing to mould responsible citizens and future leaders who live for their people and not for self.

'HRH The Nyamndom greatly frowned at moral degeneration among women because in Nyamngong the mother is the staying force of the home and country as a whole. Nyamngong is held together by cords of fraternity and love. Each belongs to the other and this chain of relationships accounts for our unity and greatness. And in this the role of women is formidable. Remember that in Nyamngong children are identified by their mothers not fathers. This underscores not only the role of women but also the high esteem in which women in Nyamngong are held. The worry now is, if the mother is coming home late and half drunk and the father is heavily drunk, what becomes of the children? Do you now see the seed of moral bankruptcy in the home and the country as a whole? You understand why HRH is so worried? If the mother and father cannot give real value to the child, that is the future generation, what legacy are we bequeathing? Where is the future of Nyamngong?

'That the old cherished ethical cultural values are no longer being upheld is worrisome and that explains why HRH had to sound the alarm bell. One of the qualities of leadership is to foresee a problem and confront it and not to lead a self-centred life or live in ignorance and nonchalance and be overwhelmed by the problem. The duty of a leader is to identify problems and solve before they become real. That is how calamities that could befall a people are avoided. HRH is a man of vision and high integrity and he cares about the wellbeing of his people and his country.

'Let me say something about duty consciousness. This is very important and I want our son to listen very attentively and apply same to his life.'

'Yes, Tar Bo, as he is now in college far away from us he can easily fall into bad hands and temptations. This is my worry. But you have said he must learn the white man's sense and witchcraft.'

'Yes, Ma Bo, we must look into the future. You have heard HRH the Nyamndom say that when he sees the growing number of young children in his Kingdom, this fills his heart with joy, thankfulness to Nyu Ngong and makes him proud of the future of Nyamngong. That is why we say *'Foo ne nwee.'* But if we only increase in numbers without growing in wisdom and moral ethics that bind us as a people, mere quantitative growth could turn out to be disastrous. We should be concerned about growth and development and not just growth.

'Duty consciousness goes with hard work, being responsible, sensitive, and honest, being creative, having the capacity to initiate and never being an eye servant. Deeply rooted in duty consciousness is time consciousness, which is doing the right thing with all your energy happily at the right time. It also means being at the right place at the right time. Whatever you have to do, do it with devotion, passion and selflessly as if the desired result, even when working with other compatriots, rested entirely on your shoulders alone. Indeed you effectively demonstrate selflessness, passion and patriotism for your country when working with others and not alone for this inspires and impacts others.

'To understand and appreciate the depth of what I am saying, let us learn from the laws of nature by this illustration I am going to make. Have you watched a hen when time is ripe for it to hatch the eggs? After having laid the eggs, when it is time for brooding, the hen spends 21 days on the eggs. The eggs have to be maintained at a particular temperature, not hot, average and cold, but regular so that the young develop and the shell cracks open for it to come out strong and healthy. The eggs undergo a process of transformation in conformity with natural law. Within this period of incubation the hen sacrifices greatly by sitting on the eggs for it knows that if it fails to maintain a regular temperature sanctioned by the law of nature the eggs will spoil. On the other hand it is regularly on the eggs to protect them against enemies, namely, human beings, dogs, snakes and other invaders. Self-survival in dignity, procreation, and protectionism are all laws of nature. You can also watch ants at work with soldiers protecting the workers and see the solid anthill they build with complex chambers. It may be the white man learnt from ants how to build story buildings with so many rooms.

'Know that Nyu Ngong did not create man to sit around doing nothing. That is why he gave man hands, feet, eyes, ears, energy and above all intelligence. With intelligence and moral consciousness man knows what is good and what is bad. He makes choices. If Nyu Ngong created the world then Nyu Ngong worked. It is therefore self-evident that when we work we are not only following the example of our Creator, Nyu Ngong, we are doing what is right and noble.

'To do the right thing at the right time has so much to do with desired results, your mind set, effectiveness, efficiency and your deep sense of integrity. What harvest will the farmer who plants maize in June or July make when the right planting season is late February and early March? But if when conscious farmers are tilling and preparing their farms in December and January for planting in February-March and another farmer

55

like a butterfly is jumping from one sweet nectar to the other and till his own farm in March-April to plant when others are weeding their maize farms, will he have any good harvest when he planted at the wrong time? Will he have anything show in August-September with the farmers who were duty conscious and time conscious? When and how you invest time and energy in doing something determines the end result of your labour or fruits of your investment.

'Being duty conscious and time conscious implies that you do not indulge into seeking pleasure at the detriment of another, taking pleasure in depending on others instead of providing for your needs. As HRH said, those who indulge into alcohol consumption are the lazy ones and once they become addicted to alcohol the more they become lazy and unproductive. A lazy person or someone addicted to alcohol cannot be a good father or a successful leader. As an individual addiction to alcohol is unproductive and so is a society or nation made up of lovers of beer, wine, alcohol or people who are pleasure-seeking. A consumer society is an unproductive society. Tell me, do we know where this beer is brewed? Is it produced by us? But it is sweeping away the small money we have. How much is a bottle of beer as compared with a big calabash of palm wine which many people can drink and not only be satisfied but also discuss things in a more productive and rational manner? Go to the bar and hear the language there: indecent, raw and crude language.

'My son, know that each people have their culture and way of life. You people are growing in an age with strange influences. We want you to grow an upright person living the Nyamngong way of life governed by cultural values as you have been taught and emphasised in this discussion. This does not mean blocking your ears to good ideas and closing your eyes from seeing good things and learning from them adapt for your own good and that of your society. No society is self-sufficient. But no society or country should be a slave of another nor should it be subjected to the dictates of another.'

'Tar Bo, what you have said is very important. And I want our son to take it very serious. I have always privately warned him against joining bad company. Is it not said that a goat that does not eat cocoyam will eat if it befriends goats used to eating cocoyam? Bad company leads to learning bad habits, imbibing evil influences. He should know the family from which he comes and should always project a good image. Know that people's eyes are on you – oh!' she said shaking her finger as point of emphasis.

'Papa and Mama, I thank you very much. Your love for me is the great source of my strength. I know who I am and I am proud of whom I am. I will not fail or disappoint you.'

'My son you have spoken well. You have already heard me tell you to get the Whiteman's knowledge and witchcraft. The Whiteman has used his knowledge and witchcraft to make the motor car, aeroplane to fly like birds in the air. I want that when you acquire the Whiteman's knowledge acquire also from our people in whom Nyu Ngong has confined the knowledge of sending thunder that witchcraft and magic. With the Whiteman's knowledge combined with that acquired from our people you should produce a powerful instrument to defend Nyamngong against the Whiteman's domination and exploitation. The Whiteman's domination of Nyamngong and Fakulum and all black people of the world in general will only end with superior knowledge of a black man who produces an instrument the Whiteman cannot. You do that Nyamngong and Fakulum will become the liberator of the black man.

'This will make Fakulum not only the centre of the black world, but the centre of the universe. I want you... my son,' he said it with great emphasis with his finger pointed at

Njemucharr, 'to do greater things than your grandfather and I, your father. A successful father that I am,' he said this proudly laying his right hand on his chest, 'must nurture a son who will do greater things for his people and country.'

'Tar Bo, you have said it well. As a mother, I will do my best. My emphasis is, listen to your father. As a boy growing up to be a man, obey him. You disobey him you will live to regret. To do great things the first step is for you to walk in his footsteps. You humble yourself before your elders you will receive the best of advice from all around who hold your father and grandfather in high esteem.

'It is a woman's great pride if her first child is a son. Firstly this wins her husband's affectionate love. The son guarantees continuity of the family line and ensures that his chair in the council of elders is secured. Secondly, it becomes a great crown and the talk of all when the son in character and deeds brings honour to the family and his country. This transforms the mother into a giant and hero. You know it is in the nature of woman to make capital out of every good situation. That also explains why we weep and mourn much, why we easily get devastated when it turns sour and very proud and rejoice much when great achievement is won and victory is attained.'

'Eh Ma Bo,' exclaimed Ta Nformi Birr, 'I never knew such great wisdom is buried within your bosom. Indeed, until the wind blows you can never the see the anus of the fowl. Thank you, you make me proud. Received wisdom has it that even the smallest bird has its gizzard.'

'Tar Bo, you too. I have grown mature' she said laughing heartily her girlish laughter of yester year. 'You think I am still the shy, simple and innocent girl, when my father gave me to you? My childishness used to make me shy before you and other men so I could not talk much. Not so again. I am a woman and a mother.' And they all laughed their lungs out.

'Papa and Mama, thank you very much for the confidence you both have in me. It makes me feel great and proud of you. You have opened the sky and assured me that that is my limit. I will do my best as Nyu Ngong sustains me and gives me the wings.

'But Papa, there is something I want you to explain to me. Why did HRH the Nyamndom demand that people should take the oath?'

'That is a good question. You remember when you were still a kid you saw the 'Bie Birr' and asked me what it was and its use.'

'Tar Bo, he asked you that?'

'Yes. He was then just three or three and half at most.'

'And what did you do?'

'You expect that I should have told him a lie? I told him the truth. It is a weapon of self-defence against enemies of the land. If your country is not under the control of the owners as bestowed by Nyu Ngong, you have no rights and place of honour; you are just a phantom.'

'And you said such hard things to a suckling, Tar Bo?'

'Papa, Mama will make you stray off my question.'

'No! I can't forget. HRH the Nyamndom is the eyes and the mouth piece of the people. He is the symbol of unity, peace, stability and to play this role he must promote justice and peace. Truth and justice are the sustaining foundation of enduring peace in society. The oath we took serves as the people's testament against any individual who goes against the people's inherent right and will. By taking the oath the people invoke the wrath of Nyu Ngong on whoever betrays them and their land. By the oath the people pledge their loyalty to the throne to, in unity and solidarity, defend their heritage.'

'Is it true that anyone who betrays will die instantly?'

'Yes, Nyu Ngong will strike him dead with his intestines gushed out. A traitor can't escape the wrath of Nyu Ngong. Treachery is an abomination and Nyu Ngong never forgives for that goes against divine will for a people. When you betray a people, you betray Nyu Ngong and his ordained will for humanity.

'You see Tar Mangong implored his people not to indulge into consumption of beer and spirits for once you are drunk your reasoning faculties are deadened. Have you seen a drunk staggering on the road? Singing meaningless songs and shouting at the wind? Come next day and ask him if he will remember anything. So my son, have no love for beer and do not crave for spirits and those imported wines even if sweet. Even the sweetness will turn bitter as the brain and nerves are sooner than later affected.'

'Yes Tar Bo, you have not said all.'

'What have I forgotten, Ma Bo?'

'You have not warned him about these girls of nowadays. I am afraid oh!'

'Yes my son in addition to staying away from beer, cultivate no love for women. Girls will fall for you because you are handsome and intelligent. Also know that your background serves as strong credentials too for attraction.

'One other thing for young men is cigarettes. Some young men indulge into such as a sign of maturity. That is dangerous. Anything that can distract you should be avoided at all cost. You have a duty to perform for your family, for your country and humanity in general and for Nyu Ngong who created you and sent you here at this point in time. Nyu Ngong does nothing inadvertently. The future of the world is in his palm.' And he said this dramatically tapping is left palm with his right index finger.

'Thank you Papa for explaining to me why the oath and the hidden message therein.'

'Yes my son, all said and done, know that the greatest heroes, patriots are born in the family. What I mean is that the foundation of great achievement, patriotism that works for national glories and honours is in the home. The seed that produces national honour germinates within the four walls of the family. No one becomes a patriot, a nationalist, a hero who was never a child that made the parents proud. Njemucharr the challenge is yours and I know you will be equal to the task.'

'Papa you said something about HRH the Nyamndom being the eyes and mouth piece of the people. I have many times heard you the elders say that HRH has one thousand eyes. What does that mean? Is he a super being?'

'My son that is a very good question and I will explain to you. Unlike the colonial Governor and those that work with him, HRH is not a foreigner. He is a prince and son of the soil. He was chosen from among the princes based on his character, sense of integrity and proven commitment to the development of Nyamngong. He ascended the throne by the collective will of the people via the king makers, the secret institutions and the laws of the land. He did not impose himself on the people. You need to know that before he made that declaration there was broad based consultation and discussion, the decision was taken as to what should be done and he was empowered to assemble the people for the declaration and the oath. Do you ever see HRH the Nyamndom in the market, in the bar or in the church or other ordinary gatherings? But how does he know all that happens around? The thousand eyes which HRH is said to have, is the entire population he governs, the living and the living-dead. In this, the spirits which we do not see are not excluded. What the people see, what they hear, even their dreams, they bring everything to the throne which is the symbol of authority. So when HRH the Nyamndom speaks, he speaks the people's will in defence of their supreme interest and that of future generations. He does not speak for himself.'

'Papa, Papa, the red cock will kill the one you bought in the market the other day. They are fighting and blood is coming out from their heads. I have separated them yet they are fighting again.' Beri, the daughter of Nformi Birr's second wife ran in complaining breathlessly.

'Who removed the cock just bought from the basket? It has not yet gotten used to the house.'

'Tar Bo, is that why they are fighting? You know even if you kept it in that basket for one month the day it is realised the one that has been in the house will still attack it. They will have to fight whether you like it or not.'

'Ma Bo, you have not answered the question I asked?'

'Tar Bo, are you the one who takes care of the chickens? Do you know how many chickens we have in this house?'

'Ok, Ma Bo, let's leave that. I know they are all under your care. I admired that big cock and bought it to await your father's visit in the next two days. That is why I did not want it to be released out. I wanted it to leave the basket only for the pot for my father-in-law. My son let us go and catch it quickly. It could be killed or forced to escape into the bush for dear life and my effort would have been wasted.'

'Papa, do not worry. I will go and catch it.'

'I know why I want to go with you.'

'My son of the two cocks which is bigger?'

'The white one you just bought.'

'Papa but why is it that whenever a new cock is brought into the compound, there will always be a fight between the new comer and the one that had been in the house?'

'Good question, my son. That is exactly why I came out with you. There are natural laws which we humans must learn and respect. Nyu Ngong, the omnipotent and omniscient has a purpose for putting these laws. If animals, birds, are bound by them should human beings who are rational not respect them more?'

'Certainly human beings should respect and defend them more, Papa.'

'Now listen. You know our red cock was hatched here. Its mother was also hatched here. From egg to chick and now a cock it has lived all its life here and produced many other chickens not only for us but for other people. In reality from the first hen this cock is the fourth generation. Therefore of the two which one knows this house and more about the house?'

'Obviously, it is the red cock that was hatched here and could as well as trace its genealogy to the fourth or fifth generation in this compound. This white one though bigger has just come.'

'Good. Of the two which one can rightly claim ownership of this house and yard?'

'Without doubt, it is the one whose history, from egg to full grown cock and beyond, is all wrapped up in this compound.'

'Do you know how the trouble began?'

'I think the red cock does not just like the white cock.'

'No, it is not so my son! It is not the issue of mere hatred or unjustified hatred. The white cock provoked the ugly situation by crowing. The red cock that grew here knows that it owns this territory. And when it crows here others answer within their given territories. But today a cock within his territory opened its beak and announced its presence. So the rightful owner attacked asking, who are you? Who has given you the right to crow here? The fight is legitimate in self-defence. It is to force the new comer to know its limits, surrender and submit to the authority of the owner of the territory or withdraw completely to its own sphere of influence for peace to reign. Without this, there will be no peace because truth is not respected and there is no justice.

Chapter Seven

For more than three years since Njemucharr entered college, the fever of 'national liberation!' anti-colonialist struggle, freedom! Independence!' among others, had reached its highest peak. Indeed what began in a small village hut under the umbrella of 'Committee of Friends' had gathered momentum and like the harmattan fire had swept across the land with unprecedented speed that the colonial repressive machinery could not hold back. Musicians of all kinds formed songs in their tongues to propagate the message for the new dawn. Nationalist leaders, some from faraway lands, were touring kingdoms and chiefdoms preaching the gospel of emancipation through a united front.

The air was charged with political rallies and campaigns everywhere. There was no weekly market in any of the villages in which sellers and buyers did not have to suspend their activities at one point or the other to listen to the nationalist leaders. Nyamntoh, the Palace of the Kingdom, was venue of frequent meetings between the political leaders and elders of the kingdom. Those from different lands, who could not speak Lingong, spoke through others. Today it is this leader and tomorrow the other, so ran the eight-day week. But the message was the same, 'There is an aggressor in the house who has turned the owner into his bond servant. This is unacceptable. He must be flushed out, come what may. You never abandon your house or bed room to a snake that has curled itself on your bed. You get a stick and shout for help. You must dispossess the aggressor and invader to repossess what legitimately belongs to you.

This land of our ancestors belongs to us and our descendants. We must not surrender to a foreign power...To surrender is not only to make our descendants slaves, it is betrayal of the will of Nyu Ngong, the supreme God.'

The entire kingdom was electrified with the message of a grand rally at the Court Yard of the People.' That early morning the mother-drum was beaten, 'Du-du-du Tfum! Tfum! Du-du-du Tfum! Tfum!' It sounded three times as the Nwentu beat it with what looked like the hand of a giant. The immediate surroundings vibrated and the sound echoed and re-echoed far and wide.

All the roads towards Nyamntoh became alive. People poured in from all over Nyamngong and Ndatamabeb. The men trooped in a warlike mode, armed with large spears, sheath machetes and traditional bags. In Nyamngong, a man does not go about without his bag which contains his cup and kola nuts, and his sheath machete and spears or at least a walking stick. These constitute the normal dressings of a man, most especially a titled man or a noble. He is always armed. This is the evidence of his manliness; prove of him as defender of his country at the hour of need. Thus approaching a house you could easily say if it was boys, women assembled in or it was men by the evidence of groups of spears lined outside against the wall of the house. But on this occasion some had even removed their war shields and dusted them. Those who had fought the **Bara mnya** remembered the war songs and their blood ran hot. The gathering concerned the identity and destiny of a people and their country. This was not a simple and light matter

By the time the sun had risen into the sky, many had arrived, while any still on the way hastened up to avoid being asked if he had been breastfeeding the baby. Remarks of this nature undermined one's manliness and quickness of mind and every man, most especially titled men avoided such comments at all cost. Even though women were respected, a titled man was better dead than being referred to as a woman. In Nyamngong roles are well defined and women do not go to war though they do the great job of feeding and nursing the sick and wounded and even discretely gathering information. The Nyamngong hold their divine role of procreation in such high esteem and see the loss of one woman in war as a big setback which must be avoided.

Before midday every beholder concluded that, except for the aggressors and their agents, every living soul was at the Court Yard of the People. And indeed it was filled to capacity; the sea of human beings spread far beyond. The innocent grass underneath strong feet suffocated thirstily as if it was responsible for foreign domination and colonial rule.

Njemucharr, who was on long holidays, watched with patriotic admiration the eagerness, anxiety and determination written on every face! Watching the crowd from a distance, it was as if one were watching a motionless sea. To be in the full picture, Njemucharr had carried his father's stool. He stood by his father, who in his distinguished position, sat in the front row. Nothing could have pleased Nformi Birr more than this and he inwardly congratulated himself.

Hon. Bongbih, the first to climb the makeshift rostrum, did so amidst thunderous applauds. Overwhelmed by the turn out, he beamed with delight and confidence. After greeting HRH the Nyamndom and elders, he turned and waved in salutation with both hands to the north, east, west and south. After welcoming all, he introduced the nationalist leaders, beginning with Comrade Monofamba of Ndatamabeb.

After motioning for attention from all the four corners of the globe, he adjusted his traditional embroiled flowing gowns with the moon distinguishingly on the back. And greeted:

'Mbaley!'

And the mammoth crowd, happily yelled, 'Bong abee!'

'Mbaley!!'

'Bong abee!'

'Mbaley!!!'

'Abee yu ngir!'

'Our elders, my people! Our gathering here today is unique and timely. It is unique in the sense that we have shun our inglorious past and gathered here as one people, victims of foreign aggression, occupation and divide and rule tactics. As we suffer the same pains, inflicted on our bodies, souls and consciences, our survival and dignity will be measured by our unreserved commitment to unity and solidarity. Received wisdom from our elders hold that even spiders in solidarity, will with their curb webs, strangle a lion to death'.

'Secondly, today and here we are laying a solid foundation for posterity which in one spirit, no force, no matter how great, shall destroy it.

'Thirdly, it is unique; for we have firmly identified the sole cause of our servitude in the midst of plenty, namely: our enemy and occupier of our land who; diabolically applying the policy of divide and rule, has turned us apart and imposed his rule and agents to lord over us. This we must overcome. And the time is now!

'Finally, it is unique; for we have come to grips with the genesis of our problem, the cancer of treachery and must henceforth bury internal hostility, blackmail, backstabbing, finger-pointing syndrome which obscures our vision and weakens the moral authority we have as the legitimate heirs of this land. To be free of our fettered chains, the shackles on our feet, there can be no choicest moment in our history than now! We must cherish the things that unite us and ignore those that divide us most especially the make believes by our colonizer. His diabolic tactics must be exposed and we must hate him who by his policies has reduced us to sub humans.'

He paused as if lacking what next to say. But it was to survey his audience and assess the impact of his speech.

Satisfied, he picked on a more deadly note.

'To understand our present predicament, let us take a step backwards. The white man believes that because of his colour, scientific and technological knowledge, his success in imposing his rule over us, he is superior. Our wealth is plundered, our women defiled with impunity, our youths slaughtered like disease infested animals; we are enslaved and denied the right to shape our destiny.

'That has been our fate, the fate of Nyamngong, Ndatamabeb and all other colonial territories. Indeed, conflict, unfounded bitter distrust and animosity have been our trade mark while the foreigner has been gathering the spoils. We have hunted each other as a hungry cat hunts the rat it smelled.

'But we must remember that a goat does not get angry with the rope tied on its neck, but with the person who put the rope on its neck and tied it to a stake. When a goat is resisting being tied, it goes after the man with its horns and not the rope.

'Does a stranger deny his host the right over his property and personal dignity?' he asked in a hoarse voice and waited for an answer. Does the stranger have the right to deny the host his liberty and happiness?

'No!' came the mournful chorus answer from the crowd. In front of him and all about him was a sea of bowed heads, mechanically in grieve and humiliation shaking from side to side.

'I see that you are grieved and broken with the little I have told you. But remember, neither tears nor lamentations will save us and set us free from this bondage. We must as a people, ask and answer this question, who are we? Did God create us to be slaves to any foreign occupier? Have any other people right over us and our land, or to make us his toys? Do we suffer from the cancer of dependency that we cannot stand on our own feet? Are we cursed to forever be the under- dogs to other people? Why should the white man decide what we should be, where we should belong and who should rule us?

'On us the aggressor and occupier has imposed his culture, traditions, laws, and his barbaric rule as if we have none. We have become his bounds men to do his bidding. He controls our land and plunders our resources for his good while like slaves we wallow in abject poverty and misery in the midst of plenty.'

Hon. Bongbih pronounced the phrase 'abject poverty' with distaste twisting his mouth as if the words tasted bitter and sour. Such emphasis sent home the message.

'This is our tragedy which, for the sake of the unborn children, we must resolve to overcome. History has no place for any people or generation that surrenders to alien rule. History does not forgive any generation that abdicates its responsibility to future generation. History never smiles at those who deny themselves their rightful place in history and among the free people of the world. The subjugated have no place of honour in human history.

'To get him off our backs and his repressive laws, ACTION, MEANINGFUL FOCUSED ACTION, is the only answer. For assuring victory, I call for unity of purpose, loyalty and irrevocable dedication to the national struggle for dignity and independence. Our right to freedom, justice and equality is non-negotiable, for God created all men equal and gave each people their land, their inheritance. This land belongs to us and no other people else.'

He went further to remind them of his speech at the school, and his comment on Njemucharr's excellent performance which challenged the long held notion of white supremacy. To the Nyamngong, he reminded them of their

70

bravery, their marvelous deeds in the past, and calling on them to invoke the same patriotic spirit for national glory. 'The lions, tigers and buffalos of yesterday in our land are not dead. They did not give birth to toothless bull dogs.' Hon. Bongbih ended on a sharp reminder to those for whom the message was meant.

In consultation among the leaders, it was agreed that the next national grand rally should take place in Covtoria. It was to be preceded by a planning meeting in Kumboya. This national grand rally was christened the Union of Forces Rally.

As people retired from this rally, every mind was alert. The message was very clear. They have lost their dignity because they are victims of foreign domination and alien rule. They are poor because their resources are exploited, looted and proceeds used for the wellbeing of the foreigner who is ruling and using the proceeds for the development of his country in Europe. Even the taxes they pay, nothing is used for the development of their country because they have no control over nor do they even know how much income comes in. One elder concluded, 'That is why as a mark of rebellion in Lingong, tax is called *'mbah ma'* (money thrown away). As a subjugated people under foreign rule we do not participate in decision making, so how could we know what is done with our money', a group of elders sipping palm wine queried as they reflected deeply. This made them to see collaboration with the enemy as treachery. 'We should take note of all our sons and daughters who are working with the colonialists who refuse to cooperate with us. Any who fails to identify with us is an enemy.'

'No! They are more dangerous said another. Is it not said that rain water cannot enter the house unless there is a hole on the wall?'

71

'Yes. But I think, the approach we should take is to do everything possible to let them see reason in the struggle for freedom and independence. We should not act stupidly to drive them into the waiting arms of the enemy. We should draw them in tactfully. We should strategically make those working with the enemy our eyes and ears. Is that not how we talk of our politicians in parliament? They know what we outside do not know.'

'You have said it all. That is the right approach. It is with such an open approach that we will know who is with us and for us and who is not with us and against us. Any one on the other side is with the enemy and for the enemy. That is the traitor. There is no midway; no neutrality. You are either for truth and justice with the people or against and with the enemy. Nyu Ngong knows how he deals with traitors and their families as it was with Achan in the bible,' complemented Pa John who was so familiar with the Whiteman's religion to the amusement of all.

With decision taken Hon, Monofamba set out to make the Grand National Rally in Covtoria historic. He toured all the chiefdoms mobilising the people to turn up for the rally. To the numerous chiefdoms whose fertile farmlands were appropriated by the first colonists and turned into huge commercial farms to boast the economic power of the Whiteman he had an appealing message –'Once the enemy is chased out, you will be your own master. What you lost will be restored.' Nothing could be more exciting and give hope to a people rendered destitute than this.

Chapter Eight

It was indeed a Grand National rally. Fixed for a Sunday afternoon, the time was so ideal. Those working with the colonial administration, in the plantations, in schools, were enthusiastic to be part of the history making event. In the past absences from work had earned them a cut in their slave wages, this was never going to be the case. They happily turned up in their numbers.

While the chiefs, notables who lost shrines and ancestral lands and farmers looked forward for some restitution, the plantation labourers and domestic servants of the white men who were so poorly paid were anxious for independence when their own brothers would be in charge and there would be no racist line for poor treatment of the blacks. As for chiefs and farmers who lost their ancestral lands they believed independence would restore them to their land and even if the plantations were not handed over to them, the money would be used to develop their country, their own children will be employed as the big men to earn huge salaries and at least the undeveloped lands will be given back to the rightful owners of the land. This was legitimate and justifiable hope and any sacrifices were seen as worthy and noble.

The plantation labourers who came from all parts of FAKULUM Territory and some neighbouring African territories constituted the true barometer of nationalism, patriotism and the urgency for independence. There were the proletariat whose hard labour on meagre wages created the fabulous sums for the plantation owners. By their profuse sweat and long hours of back breaking labour sometimes added with the cane, the white capitalist plantation owners, like ticks sucked the blood of African labourers and the inhabitants in general. These labourers, who labour at the pleasure of the white capitalists, produce what the capitalist desire. They are treated sub humanly and receive nothing commensurate with their labour while the master reaps surplus value for his good and that of his country in colonising FAKULUM whose large chunks of land had been ceased from the natives at gun-point. While the labourers or the proletariat have no control over what they produce and know not how much they produce, the white capitalists impose slave wages to maximise gain and boost the economic might of their metropolitan nation in Europe. What needs be understood here is that colonial powers constitute a club against colonised Africa for the prestige and splendour of Europe so they collaborate and synchronise their strategies against the subjugated in Africa.

Though the proletariat works so hard and produce so much, they do not benefit from the fruit of their labour. As declared subjects of grim exploitation, the firm grip of poverty on them had become their identity card. Though it pains them much and it was revolting and they within their circles discussed their misery and helplessness with bitter agony they were condemned to clutch tenaciously to this kind of labour for they had no alternative source of employment. They accepted the slave wage to escape starving to death with their families.

Though the plantations were owned by individual white capitalists, to the natives these blood thirsty foreigners did not only look alike physically, their hearts, minds and spirits were same against the black man. The condition of the labourer is made worse by the fact that these capitalists appropriated their fertile lands from their forebears who were rendered destitute on forcefully losing their ancestral lands. The loss of ancestral land meant total denial to practice peasant agriculture, hunting and carrying out of other arts they were used to for decent survival. They became a dependent people. The rugged country side they were chased to was completely unsuitable for any kind of agriculture. This is structural violence which has decapitated the people. The invader has not only confiscated their inherent rights to their development morally, culturally, socially, economically and intellectually, by dispossessing them of their inheritance they have been made a permanent captured people. Dispossession of their ancestral land and having their shrines destroyed is more than an economic factor: this is married with political and religious factors; it is destroying the soul of a people's nation. The people suffer from a disconnect with their past for their roots have been cut off. This is like removing a fish from the Atlantic Ocean and expecting it to survive in the Sahara Desert, procreate and prosper.

The psychological trauma the natives suffered was manifested in their rebellion to work as labourers on such slave wages. Only a negligible few of the natives worked in the plantations. Regarding those who worked as labourers as **nkwa bara** they preferred safeguarding what remained of their dignity in poverty to enslaving their souls for slave wage. That, to them was insult too much to bear. The plantation owners who could not understand their sense of dignity and judgement and had to import labour from other tribes of the territory, they dismissed the natives as pathologically lazy people who indulged into drinking, gossiping and complaining and dreaming of a glorious yesterday in tears which they could never recover, the plantation owners concluded mockingly.

The plantation labourers had much to complain about and seeing independence, which to them meant ending the white man's control of the plantations and naked exploitation of the Fakulum people in particular and the African in general, they were ready to take whatever action was needed. To these they saw independence as redemptive to end destitution and to build the new man with a new consciousness and dignity.

Students and even parents who had children in colleges were so excited about the prospect of independence when the Whiteman rule will be over and sons and daughters of the land will take over and rule in various capacities and development will be expedited. Njemucharr and his colleagues who attended the rally in Nyamntoh, Nyamngong were like tutors to those who had never had the experience. In eloquent narration Njemucharr kept his friends thrilled with last rally's message and why it was necessary that they the expected future leaders should be enthusiastic about what was happening and should be actively involved and make their contribution to the struggle for independence.

All these expectations and hopes kindled interest in the Grand National Rally which was christened Union of Forces. As independence promised new dawn, the message spread like wild fire and support and commitment to unite and work for freedom and independence attracted all interest groups to the fold. Expectations were indeed high, justifiable and legitimate living no one in doubt as to the benefits of independence to the owners of the land.

The nationalist crusader of Ndatamabeb, Monofamba, described as a speaker with lashing flames of fire in his mouth, in his marathon speech likened the situation between Ndatamabeb and Nyamngong to a well-known folk tale in all the kingdoms and chiefdoms of the territory about the villain tactics of a cunning animal called Takweh.

'Takweh in his deceit, tact, avarice and boastfulness', he went on, 'made bait with the largest land animal, the Elephant, and the largest sea animal, the Hippopotamus, challenging each to polling contest with him, Takweh.

'My people,' he addressed the sea of human beings, 'as you all know, instead of personally engaging in the pulling contest as he boasted, he tricked the two large animals into pulling each other without knowing. At the shaking of the rope as agreed with each, the tugging began and went on, and on, and on. Each wondering how Takweh could be so strong and determined to teach small Takweh a lesson, each put in all its tactics and energy. Finally the two equally being so strong both dropped down dead, the one by the sea and the other far on land. Takweh declared himself the conqueror of each after having fought no war. His diabolic trick did the job and the innocent fought to death. All what belonged to the Elephant and Hippopotamus, respectively, became Takweh's. Takweh declared himself the strongest animal on land and sea. He proclaimed himself the conqueror and the innocent strong animals the vanquished.'

Then he paused, adjusted his gowns and with his huge finger drained down sweat from his face. As his eyes surveyed the human sea each of the thousand minds was buried in search of a meaning and tried to relate it to one thing or the other. Indeed, with a moral intense search, a new image was unveiling before the countless eyes, minds and souls. But all knew the speaker was not yet done and were anxious to hear him land.

Njemucharr by his father was also searching his small inquisitive mind. He watched and saw that the man's hands were shaking akin to a person who stammers quivering for action when his lips refuse to pronounce a verbal attack on the enemy. 'Indeed he is...' Njemucharr's thoughts were cut short as the speaker raised his hands for attention.

'Elders, my brothers and sisters' he continued, 'this story points practically to our fate today. The Elephant and Hippopotamus represent Nyamngong and Ndatamabeb who were tricked into quarreling, distrusting and suspecting each other, fighting each other, betraying each other to the common enemy and dying for nothing. Takweh is the foreign occupier of our land who lives on deceit, treachery, corruption, patronage, repression and wanton exploitation. He uses the carrot and the stick with reckless abundance. He may smile with you from ear to ear but he trusts none of us. You are relevant to him in as much as you betray your own kind. In defense of his interest none of us is worth more than the toilet roll he uses to clean his nyash.'

The equation of human beings with toilet roll was so irritating and vexing that some felt throwing out. With this illustration they saw their tragic loss of self-dignity under foreign domination and alien rule.

'Today, unlike before', Hon Monofamba went on; 'we are divided and ruled by his agents. We are poor, wretched and enslaved, because our fathers were tricked and our land occupied. We must not continue to suffer forever. Remember, every human product has its expiration date buried in its bowels. But we are condemned to work and hasten this expiration.

'We must as a people, conscious of our being and self-worth, determined to lead and shape our destiny, rise up and end this foreign domination and servitude. The time has come and it is now! There are only two options before us all; to liberate ourselves or to remain the slaves of the foreign dictator. But what moral justifications have we to enslave our children and our children's children? We must STOP IT NOW!' and he thrust his clenched fist so furiously as if to end it all with his clenched fist.

'Elders, sons and daughters of Nyamngong and Ndatamabeb, where are those among you with seven eyes? Where are those who see up and see down? Where are the spirit killers and those before whom bones melted? In the days gone by we had men who defiled the rains, the scorching inferno, the harmattan and tornado for the cause of justice and human dignity and to save lives. These counted themselves last and the collective interest foremost and supreme. My people did such tigers, leopards and lions of the good old days give birth to lame lambs? How does a true man fail to strike back when challenged in his own house or when unjustifiably spat upon in the face? How does a man worthy of that name watch his own wife or daughter defiled and he smiles and dines with the enemy?'

This was followed by a long pause, of anxiety and soul searching. It left every heart boiling with rage.

'We cry for unity to ensure that we move out in one spirit and to ensure that there are no traitors amongst us. Indeed it is to ensure that there is no enemy in the house. With him in the house, the spirit of the struggle leaks. Our enemy is he who is against our interest, our inherent right to freedom, equality and dignity, our collective survival in dignity as a people; irrespective of colour, culture and language.

'Why do we name a son Wepnjeh? Is it that we want him to be a coward? Or we want him to suffocate under the weight of fear? Why? Tell me.' And he surveyed the huge crowd with a curious eye.

'It is because the people are supreme. No individual is above the collective will and interest of the people,' answered Ta Nformi Birr.

'Thank you, offspring of he who caught lions and leopards with bare hands. Thank you, the people's pride who drinks from a white skull. That answer sums up everything.....' remarked the Speaker, Hon. Monofamba.

'Remember he who takes over and controls your land, imposes his laws, changes your history, becomes your maker and you his bondsman. You become a people without a past worthy to be remembered. Your great ancestors cease being, for you have no past. And above all, your descendants are born slaves and they live in servitude forever. This is our fate and the fate of our descendants if we surrender. Thus we are condemned to right this before it becomes too late' Monofamba concluded receiving prolonged applause.

Hitherto men regarded folklore as entertainment for women and kids, but here was a man painting a new picture, using a well familiar tale as good straw to present a new image. In his well-intended analogy he drew a clear demarcating line between the people with their inherent rights to their heritage, and the invader and colonizer, who by force and intrigues, has reduced the owners of the land into serfdom. If by fighting among themselves the foreign aggressor got richer and they poorer, if by fighting and killing themselves, they got fragmented and weaker and the enemy stronger, if by remaining divided, they enslaved themselves under the yoke of the aggressor and occupier: the right moment had come for them to cease from turning their spears inward and in solidarity turn them outward against the arch enemy, the dictator, oppressor and exploiter. They clearly saw at work the trick, the policy of divide and rule which made it easy for the invader to cheaply realise his goal, to be master and lord of a people weakened by imposed internal division, assimilation and cultural dilution, strive, distrust and plunder of their natural wealth.

In Monofamba's political speeches, he lashed so furiously at the colonial rulers and their local agents in the army, civil service and the collaborators in business who exploited the masses to enrich their external mentors. It was said that even the colonialists recognized and envied his leadership qualities, admired his will-power drive and dreaded the charging power of his speeches which had a kind of spell power over his audience. Anyone who heard him left the place determined to act in good faith for the good of all. His words lashed out at the enemy just as the fangs of the poisonous large snake leave the victim stiff instantly on the ground.

All his opponents feared him and the colonialists who did not want to lose grip of their mines, estates and cheap labour saw the solution only in the physical liquidation of Monofamba. But the history of revolutions had taught them that physical elimination of such powerful leaders had never been a solution either in the short or long term.

When the people had heard all that he revealed to them, their blood went hot from within. Even the canny were resolved to fight it out since that was the only option. Ta Nformi Birr, the Commander of Nyamngong army, though now only in name, saw this as an opportunity to revive and reassert the military honour of his family genealogy. His father Tatah Ngoh had become army general at the tender age of twenty-nine and a mere mention of his name sent men in enemy camps messing in their loins. He was a terror, and like lightening he struck fatally when necessary. Though the kingdom was deprived of him so early as a result of colonial intrigues, he had brought home more heads and captives in chains than all the generals before him put together. In fact, he was the first black general to bring home a white head from a battlefield.

The negative effects of the white man's rule were not new to the Nyamngong, Nformi Birr and all the members of the royal family. In the war against the 'Bara mnya' the Nyamngong, under the military expertise of their army commander Tatah Ngoh, fought gallantly. Their stubborn resistance so much provoked the anger of the invaders to their bones, challenging the myth of their invulnerability, and they decided to attack the palace in full force. They entered the shrines, looted valuable property, setting shrines they feared to enter ablaze. But as they did not reach Nyamngai, Ndapngong remained undestroyed.

But the army general was arrested, tied to a stake, and shot in the head in the presence of weeping women and terrified children, who were forced to stand and watch.

Tatah Ngoh, on dying, told his people in Lingong that he was dying a hero because he had fought and killed white men and traitors in defense of his country and his people's right to freedom, justice, and human dignity. 'We were neither born in chains and shackles nor to be the footstool of any people, black, brown or white. If you worship them, in the hope of survival, you will forever remain slaves. You can't afford to betray our descendants. You will by so doing betray the cause for which we have died. To bring about meaningful change and live in dignity, we must discipline fear which betrays our humanity. Whatever you do, please remember that, we are below watching you. Rain water will come and inform us below. Remember, an enemy is always an enemy. Remember also that those who die and vanish from the conscience of men are those who betray the will of the people. But those who defend their land and the collective will of the people, even if they die, they live forever. We live in deeds not in days. When a man dies, his good deeds stand in his honour as a tomb stone. We must live together for a cause, and if death is the inevitable price for the general good, it is not too great a price to pay. Goodbye.'

With these last words pronounced, he was shot seven times in the head before he died. Tangkoh, his first son, who succeeded him as Nformi Birr got the last words from his father in hot tears. It was a hard experience and he knew fully well that his beloved father, a man he had grown to love, respect, adore and fear, died prematurely not because he unjustifiably hated the white man but because he loved his country and people most. He uncompromisingly hated the gross injustice done his people. He paid the supreme price for freedom and for defending the sovereignty of his kingdom, Nyamngong. He died in defense of a universal ideal.

.

Chapter Nine

Nformi Birr, sitting on the stool inherited from his forebears heard all what Hon. Monofamba had said. He had listened with revived interest in Hon. Bongbih's speech and the eulogy and glorious tributes paid to his late father, Tatah Ngoh, his grandfather HRH the Nyamndom who had defied the threats of the white man three times and resisted his expansionist aggression for seven long years. Hon. Bongbih in his speech also made clear recount of his mother's father, Nfapmbeh, who as the army general of the Nyamngong, routed all invaders setting them in retreat in panic and disarray.

It was said that Tatah Ngoh, his father, on becoming the army general after Nfapmbeh was crowned Fai Ndingah Nwenfu, combined in him the courage and fierceness of the lion in his father-in-law with the high leadership expertise, devotion, integrity, organizational skill, high intelligence and power of speech of his father, HRH the Nyamndom who ruled ten decades ago. It was therefore no surprise that he succeeded so well. People expected great things from him and he gave, not just what they expected, but more.

To Nformi Birr, both Hon. Monofamba and Hon. Bongbih were speaking directly to him, and he got the message. They were directly asking him if he had become the archaeological wood-ash long forgotten under ancient settlements. He turned this question in his mind over and over and finally heard a new person rising in him, and his body getting warmer. From within, he heard a voice saying to him aloud: 'No, we must not go down on our knees. We must not become donkeys for the white man to ride on. We must rise up and straighten our backs like the men that we are and defend who we are. We must fight back in self-defense as ever before, sending the enemy packing'. And addressing him directly, the voice charged; 'And you Nformi Birr, must not lie down bleating like an old sheep while being dismembered by a wild carnivorous beast!'

As he looked steadfastly in front of him, his mind's eye saw his father on the stake and his mind's ears heard the very cold words he had heard years back when he stood sobbing and begging for his father's remains. To those statements were added: 'son of my loins, the first mark of my manhood, have you become a woman? Don't you remember?'

And unconsciously he sprang to his feet and answered 'Yes I do. I will follow your foot steps and in honour; I shall act purposefully come what may.'

The speaker, noticing this, became overwhelmed and called for perfect peace so that Nformi Birr of Nyamngong should speak to the people.

Before walking up to the make-shift platform, he gently tapped Njemucharr on his shoulders. It was this tap that brought him to life; for he had been carried away. He had been in a reverie.

Nformi Birr's speech was laconic and to the point. This was in the nature of men of action. After thanking Monofamba for his relentless efforts to liberate the country from foreign occupation, he went on to make his remarks.

'The Nyamngong and Ndatamabeb bear same frontal mark; it is the mark of victims of external aggression, foreign domination and servitude. As we are one people under subjugation, assimilation and exploitation, our only hope lies in collective struggle, for the liberation of our fatherland, Fakulum. But mark you, struggle comes with great sacrifice. It is however more honourable to sacrifice now than to assist in the entrenchment of subjugation and exploitation which will eventually cause the annihilation of our cultural heritage and extinction of Fakulum. But I want all of you here to remember one thing. There is no middle way – no ambivalence. There is no room for sitting on the fence. You are either with your people or with the enemy of your people. Either we collectively rise for our liberation or we assist the invader in our enslavement and final extermination.

'My people,' Nformi Birr went on, 'the white man and his devilish rule, aided by lackeys, are like lice infested blankets. If you want to get rid of the lice, you must not eliminate the adults leaving the eggs. You must cook the blanket in real boiling water for long in order to kill both the lice and eggs.' This analogy was greeted with great applause.

He ended up by explaining how the kings, the titled men and women had lost grip of the society, how the society had deteriorated into fragility and was collapsing like a house moulded with sand-clay mod and left unroofed under torrential rain. He cited many other vices all of which he blamed on imposition of colonial rule, foreign culture, values and religion. He lamented how under the mad rush for fashion anything foreign was the standard to be copied sheepishly.

'Do our elders not say that when the son of the soil sobs in agony the earth harkens? But how does the son of the soil sob? Is it by folding his hands? No he sobs in action. He sobs by remaining faithful to the ideals of his forefathers, his culture and traditions. He sobs by rejecting foreign domination and alien rule. He sobs by defending his personal self-worth and the collective identity of his people of which he is a living symbol.

'Why do we name a child Yuniwo? This is to say that the will of the people is supreme. That is why we say '*Fo ni nwe*' and '*abee yu ngir*.' On the other hand, although HRH the Nyamndom is highly respected and venerated, our people would say that the ruler is there because of his people. It is the collective voice, indeed the collective will that proclaims the will of the gods.

'I am fully in support of the call for unity against the enemy. The reason is simple. Do our elders not say that not even the wild harmattan fire can cross any river, unless it has a secret agent? The white-man we all blame is sitting over us, commanding us, ordering us to pay tax. He has enslaved us and is exploiting our natural resources. But would he have done so without some collaborators from amongst us? How many white men are there in Nyamngong and Ndatamabeb put together? Are we all here?' He paused and surveyed the sea of human beings that had greeted his speech with a prolonged applause and saw some shaking their heads mournfully.

'We have the most difficult task but it is not unachievable. It must be fought on all fronts. Our problem is compounded by those brothers who have become whiter than the white-man himself. If you are going out and your house is clean, you will return to it safely. If the contrary is the case, you are doomed. This is why our elders say that unless you are sacrificed or given out by your own brother, the wizards from outside cannot strike you dead. We must here resolve to stand together as one man to redeem our battered image and restore our freedom and dignity. Are we ready and determined to regain our freedom?' he rented the air with his strong voice.

'Yes we are!' came the chorus answer from the crowd.

'*Mbaley*, are we ready?' he asked again

'Yes, very ready' came the chorus answer, this time with men shaking their spears in the air.

'Thank you my people. Time has come for *Bong abee* to prove itself practically. For me I am ready. The words of the wise tell us that 'An antelope cries had I known while on the shoulder of the hunter.' It is now or never. Any failure to act in unity now shall provide us no opportunity to regret like the antelope for we shall not be us again. Once more thank you.' And he sprang down like a cat amidst applause and dancing as if the enemy has been chased out and victory has already been attained.

Njemucharr had watched the proceedings of this political rally and heard the speakers from start to finish, though it was not possible for him to understand all that was said since so much was woven into proverbs. But he gathered one thing – the people were all united against the white-man for his repressive and exploitative rule. He was an enemy. He was impressed to see and listen to Honourable Bongbih and this reminded him of the remark he made about his brilliant academic performance over white children which was likened to the imminent defeat of colonial rule. Njemucharr then saw this as his own contribution, not the widow's mite anyway, since it was a pointer to the defeat of the colonialists. He remembered vividly what he had always been told about the exceptional bravery and patriotism of his grand and great grandparents and was determined to do same in future in whatever way possible.

But the emphasis on the determination to drive away the white man made him wonder whether that was not going to mean closing down the colleges, in which case he may not be able to further his education. The possibility of making his educational prospect gloomy, held his thoughts in check. At the Imperial College where he was currently studying, the proportion of whites to black staff was fourteen to three. Worried about the implication of this, back in the house, he asked his father.

'Father,' he called respectfully, 'I was very happy to hear you speak at that political rally. I was also happy to hear what the other speakers, most especially Hon Bongbih and Hon.

Monofamba, said. But don't you think that if we drive the white man, the colleges will close down? Yet you had told me that you wanted me to get all the white man's knowledge. How will I do it then?'

'No, no college will ever close. These foreigners are very bad ones. They are ruling us and they say we are primitive and inferior because we are black. We don't want them to rule us again. Honourable Bongbih and Monofamba say that when these men go away, we shall arrange for good ones who shall come as friends to help us. Independence is very important. With freedom and independence, you will be a master in your own country, you will choose the countries with which to cooperate, in your interest make your own choices and do what is right according to your aspirations and development needs,' said his father.

Njemucharr reasoned over what his father said and saw the white man's discrimination and disregard for the black man. What made him shudder was the white man's colour line which was practiced even in the church. What readily came to his mind was the case of black women forbidden from coming to church without a headgear on grounds that it was wrong or a sin, but he had never seen a white woman covering her hair or wearing a headgear in the church.

Convinced that the evidences were overwhelming, he vowed, 'I will hate social injustice, oppression, discrimination, foreign domination and anything that stands in the way of human dignity, human equality and freedom even unto death.

Chapter Ten

'Your Majesty, the Lion of Nyamngong, this meeting is strategic. Our mission here and now is to determine the way forward. The colonial master is determined not to grant us independence according to the universal rules and the wishes of our people. Independence is our right but they are imposing unacceptable conditions as we all know. Every effort to make them reason with us, to make them respect the UN Charter as they did in other countries has failed.

'Are they demanding a bribe, if I may ask? The elders say that as the elephant consumes heavily so is its excreta. But these imperialists look like their stomach is never full so they are never satisfied no matter how much they swallow.' And they all laughed sarcastically.

'And now back to business. But before we adopt a workable plan of action, it is logical that we expose and understand the diabolic tactics of the coloniser and how over the years he has tried to empty us of our being and self-worth; he has rendered us powerless through polarisation and made us irrelevant and for that whatever we say means nothing to him. We must tactfully articulate the problem. For a successful anti-colonial war, we must arouse the consciences of our people; give them political education to defend their self-worth individually and collectively.'

'Yes, Hon. Bongbih, you are our eyes and ears. You have at small meetings and big rallies recounted and recounted how obstinate and cunning this colonial master has overnight turned out to be. We had taken his smiles and gentle ways as evidence of good character. His smiles belie his true nature. I agree with you, we must find a solution to the problem. We must recover our identity and be master of our destiny.

Colonial rule must end and decolonisation must give birth to a brand new identity, namely, national sovereignty and independence.

'This meeting is strategic because we must adopt a firm plan of action. It is equally strategic because this plan of action must remain top secret known only to this conclave and Nyu Ngong who gave us this land as our heritage. People should only see things unfolding and results therefrom.'

'Yes you people have spoken well. As the chief custodian we know that Nyu Ngong, to our ancestors, declared Nyamngong our homeland and heritage. In so doing the Supreme Being did not need to consult any other god. Did he have to seek the approval of anyone or people? Why should we today on our knees beg to be free? I ask you, especially you, the Honourables; who are our eyes and ears.'

'Your Majesty, you have struck the core of the problem, namely, our identity, without which we are nothing. Since the first white man under Bismarck ruled us, my people became destitute,' Hon. Monofamba lamented gravely. Their land was appropriated. Our ancestors were, as a conquered people banished to the rocky hilly slopes of the mountain. All the fertile plains were appropriated for their commercial farms. While we lost everything the invader gained everything. As we were scattered and banished our shrines were destroyed, we were disconnected from our ancestors. Our traditional and cultural life was tampered with. We are victims of cultural obliteration. Such extreme depravity has reduced us to outcasts. To be disconnected from your roots, my people....' He was lost for words.

'When their greed and quarrels for more prestige and grandeur resulted in war in their own part of the world, they extended it here. What interest had we in a European tribal war? At the end Bismarck's country was defeated and humiliated. But we suffered worse. Like common and disposable property, we were handed over to a new European colonial power without our consent. It proved not to be different. Though the new pretended to smile often, tolerated some of our ways and customs, their hearts have never been with us. They refused to restore our land. We remained destitute. This explains the absence of cultural fibres that bind our people. With the loss of our cultural heritage and our land to the invader, the spirit of industry was killed in our people by the first European power that occupied our land. This evil has been perpetuated to this day by the successor. The fight we are engaged in must be intense and redemptive. The attack on family and community life and spirit sowed the devilish seed of individualism in our people. They were not only separated and scattered physically, they were ripped of their social and cultural identity.'

'After listening attentively to His Majesty and the two of you, our eyes, ears and mouth before the colonial ruler, I see we are left with no choice than do what is right. And what is right is that which will restore us to our inherent dignity. The role of men is not only to know their history and preserve same. To know just the history without knowing the boundaries of their country which in patriotic spirit they must defend is meaningless,' Nformi Birr insisted stamping down his foot.

'I have heard Hon. Monofamba very well. He has made a good recapitulation of the grave consequences of colonial rule on his people, land and culture. We in the upland might not have been so decapitated. But their suffering is our suffering. We cannot be free without them nor can they. We must be united and see colonial rule as an evil, a stain on our people and personality.

'Received wisdom teaches us that the early morning cock that crows to wake people up is owned by one house, but its alarm bell is welcome by all inhabitants in the neighbourhood. So is it with any good deed by one man which becomes assert for all in the community, in the country from generation to generation.

'The nation and the people are two sides of the same coin. You cannot have one without the other. You cannot say this is your country when it is controlled and mismanaged by foreigners for their good and prestige. The people who are the owners must defend it to preserve their identity and honour for without their country they lose the foundation of their being and integrity.'

'Thank you off spring of the lion of our land. Thank you all. From your well thought out and calculated interventions we are all agreed that foreign domination and alien rule is evil against the dignity of the subjugated. The imperialist present themselves as a perfect people, specially created to lord it over us. They present their culture as a superior civilisation and ours as savagery as if we were monsters. If we were monsters how would they have come to live among us? These whites lord it over us as if on our knees we came begging them to deliver us from some evil. They are the evil and their savage culture which manifests itself in monstrous greed has destroyed us and retarded our spiritual, cultural, economic, social and physical development.

'From those in the church, with their spirit of holier than thou, they paved the way for colonial rule. They behave as if the creator sent them from celestial space to come and rescue us from the claws of the enemy, Satan, to those in government, is there a difference in their attitude towards us? Yet they talk of God as the Creator of mankind and the world. If they believe in the God they preach, did God create a super race with a super culture to lord it over some humans who are inferior? Was the Dark Age we learn in history not in Europe? If they know and belief in the God they preach, God's love and spirit should manifest itself in them. They shouldn't kill others. They shouldn't destroy the culture and property of others. They should not exploit and kill others. God's law say thou shall not kill! Yet they kill to impose their rule on others. God is not a greedy and arrogant God. He is not a god of monopoly. The true God is a God of truth, love, and justice. He is the God of beauty in diversity.'

'Thank you, Hon. Monofamba, for unveiling the past and the true situation in your part of the country to us. The presence of Enow and Neba are very encouraging and inspiring. Firstly, as far as emphasis on unity of purpose is concerned, their presence and participation is very important. Secondly, talking about the resistance against colonial rule and wars against the invaders, is concerned, their ancestors are well remembered and honoured for their bravery and gallant fights against foreign domination. My brothers, you are welcome.'

'Thank you very much. We regret our late arrival. The roads are so bad and it was not even easy to get transport. We have spent two days on the road. However, it is better late than never.'

'That is part of the problem. And as I was saying, we need to have a holistic picture of the problem, circumstances under which we live, the bleak future for our children if we fail to adopt a holistic approach to the national problem for a national solution.

'Why do we in songs recount the past? The wars fought; the bravery of our warriors, heroes and kings who distinguished in battle and selfless leadership? This is not madness or arrogance and empty pride of the musician. It is to inspire the younger generation that they are not upstarts but that they are off springs of doers, people who made things happen, that they have a rich and proud history which must be preserved and defended. Such lessons are equally important to warn them against falling into temptations. With understanding they are encouraged to face today with patriotic determination in order to build a better future. Without the determination to lay a foundation today, you have nothing to look up to. To avoid blunders, we must know both the good and the bad: each situation has a lesson for the living and our descendants.

'The stories passed unto us in music or in folk tale about our ancestors, about our land, our rulers and heroes are critical, they in style set us apart from other peoples. No people duplicate another so is the history and culture of each people. Our past is very important in shaping our future. Our rich history and culture firmly place our footprints in the sands of history. Our past distinguishes us as a people within the family of the human race. Each people their land, each people their distinct story to tell and each people their carved place within the confluence of humanity. For each people to occupy their deserved place in history, they must preserve their past. However, they must in character and deed preserve the past as the spring board for a better future, without working for a better future by defending who you are the past is buried in rubbles of ignominy. It is the future achieved that sings the glories of the past that laid a solid foundation for the future. For a continuum, the past, the present and the future must be married in holy wedlock.'

'My people listen to me and listen well. Our elders teach us that the mouthy or noisy bird that makes all the promises of how beautiful his house will be never builds. But the *Kuishi bubu* sets to work with its beak noiselessly. At the end like the ants that build a huge ant hill with complex chambers, you only see a well-constructed self-contained house deep inside the trunk of a mighty tree. No one has ever doubted the ingenuity and resourcefulness of the ants on the ground and the Kuishi bubu on the tree. The actions of these two creatures tell their good story.

When Lunga, the Messenger from the Most High, the Merciful and Omnipotent, landed on the famous rock, he pronounced to us two eternal truths, namely, *Fo ne nweh* and *Abee yu ngir.* But before I go to expatiate on these two principles, let me make a statement or two on why Lunga landed on the rock where the footprints remains to this day. Why did Nyu Ngong make him land on the rock to the summit of Rtu Kaah? Is it that there was no plain or soft ground on which he could have landed?

'Your Majesty, we are all ears', said excited Enow, keenly anxious to be nourished with received wisdom passed from generation to generation. To Enow, it was a unique opportunity for him to be before His Majesty, the Nyamndom, a man of great wisdom he had heard about for long. Destiny at a most propitious moment in his life time had brought him face to face with a personality he had heard of always from a distance.

'No one in his right senses kicks a stone, let alone a rock with his foot. Lunga landed on the rock to remind the Nyamngong that the Omnipotent and Omniscient Nyu Ngong created them to be strong, brave, courageous and cunning. To be brave and courageous, demands that they should never bend their backs for others to ride on. And if you don't bend your back no one will ride you like a donkey. To be cunning demands that you should be as wise as the serpent. Once the enemy is identified you never play games with him, you never pretend and you never compromise. He who is an enemy to you today will forever remain an enemy even to your descendants to the fourth and fifth generations. He will turn your history upside down and make your descendants serve him as his slaves. I hear some among us preach that we should wait, we should exercise patience, we should pray. This is treacherous! You do not make an enemy reason by self-resignation. You make an enemy reason by proving to him that you know who he is and what his diabolic intentions are; in a word, you confront him in his own ball game.

When His Majesty landed, all took a deep breathe nodding their heads in approval.

'And back to the two philosophical principles brought to our fore bears by Lunga. '*Fo ne nweh*' simply means honour and glory in the human person. In the life of the community we are reminded that the ruler or leader is great thanks to his people and that without the people, the aura and myth making him great does not exist. It does not just mean that as the embodiment of his people, it is they who make him great; the deep meaning is that it is the people who are great.

'*Abee yu ngir*' emphasises not only the greatness in unity but the invulnerability that is inherent in unity and solidarity. *Abee yu ngir* emphasises unity of purpose, unity guarded by principles for a national cause or in defence of the people's identity and interest. This is not just theory but theory and practice bound together by history, culture and territory, the heritage which must be nourished and passed on to our descendants in whole and better than we inherited from our ancestors. *Fo ne nweh* and *Abee yu ngir* teach us one eternal truth, a universal truth of all cultures and lands, that each generation has it a bounding duty to confront diligently and solve the problem of their age. To pass on the bulk to the next generation, innocent of how the problem came about, is not only treacherous; it is to wipe off their name from history which they the generation wrote in chalk.'

Your Majesty, like the lion that you are, you have said it all. You have summed it. There is no point over labouring the point'. And he turned and asked, 'Am I speaking your mind?' and all answered. 'Yes'

'Before adopting the strategies and assigning responsibilities which must be executed diligently and with selfless patriotic spirit, permit me sum up our solemn discussions.

'Let us put an end to self-deception. There shall never be peace in this land and in the world until Truth is respected and defended with all might if need be. The Justice that we seek is not exclusive, it is inclusive. We seek Justice for ourselves as well as for all our neighbours and the entire human race. The Justice that we seek, which by natures' gift we are entitled to as of right as a people will reign only if Truth, infinite Truth, is respected and defended. We are not talking here of Truth and Justice as defined by the strong and powerful but as defined and ordained by the Creator for all creation as manifested in unity and beauty in diversity and harmony in diverse synchronised musical instruments. We are talking here of Truth and Justice as recognised, accepted, appreciated and upheld by both the strong and the weak, the big and the small. When the equality of all is solemnly respected and defended, enduring peace whose foundation is Truth and Justice for all humankind will reign. This is Truth and Justice that transforms and lifts the subjugated from the abyss of suffering, rejection and depravity to freedom, equality and happiness.

'All peoples who live the life of honour and are respected by others, have Truth as to who they are on their side. We must firmly reject this faulty and demeaning categorisation and characterisation as to who we are by those who have imposed themselves on us. Until this is done successfully, we are of no consequence to them. The subjective categorisation and name stamped on our face will become an acceptable label and will endure to our descendants. This is the challenge of the moment. We have no alternative than to face the challenge squarely.

'Our mission here is to adopt a road map as to what must be done. We must strategise what must be done to successfully defend and preserve our identity without which we cease being. In preserving our identity, what binds us together, namely, our culture, our traditions, our language, our territorial integrity, our likes and dislikes must be preserved through teaching and practice. In fighting the enemy we must love and adore our country, our people and our gods even more. We must see an attack on our past and ancestors as a deliberate action of discontent to project us as upstarts. Without our past, we have no future. Today is the child of yesterday and yesterday is the grandfather of tomorrow. No people have a perfect yesterday but each people in positive concrete effort use their yesterday and today to build a better and rewarding tomorrow. It is along these lines that positive action ensures measureable results and the transforming good of each generation is recorded and the names of heroes are engraved in gold on the rocks of human history.

In the adoption of the strategic plan of action, deliberate action to cement the unity of Fakulum was a top priority. This was to be evidenced by the adoption of common plans of action and singular efforts of the political leaders who should address national rallies together. Massive sensitisation, education and mobilisation from the grassroots was seen as the logical means of building enduring unity to counter the coloniser's policy of divide and rule. In addition to mass rallies, men and women of the sharp pen were encouraged to write for the elite and the urbanised, artists were called upon to seriously go to work and make fresh compositions of music and dance for the masses and revolutionised story telling for the young who must be given fresh orientation. This was to draw a clear dividing line between 'WE' the people and 'THEY' the enemy. While Nformi Birr's rule needed no public debate, the Natural Rulers, the politicians, the youths and the women had clear defined rules with a clear convergence point – the firm defence of TRUTH, FREEDOM, JUSTICE, INDEPENDENCE.

Chapter Eleven

In all the territory of FAKULUM, both the ruled and the ruler were gripped and subjected to a reign of tension, fear and uncertainty. As much as one could not say when, how and from which direction hell would break loose, one thing was most obvious, it was too late to prevent the inevitable. The atmosphere was so menacingly charged. Evidently, even the colonialists had given up the determination to track down and nib in the bud those involved. The uneasy calm was too traumatizing that everyone wondered what would happen when the explosion would take place. It was a state of hopelessness.

Preparations for the total uprising to dismantle the colonial machinery were carried out in absolute secrecy. Under the command of Nformi Birr there was witchcraft and magic married into one. Both the training and meetings were held in the forest and when in operation, the forest ceased to be part of this physical world; it became a world of its own, perfectly sealed off from human view. Indeed, even telescopes could not pierce through nor could the helicopters hovering above with individuals armed with field glasses could locate the camps below.

A month to the nationwide attack, there was a grand meeting of all the command units. Comrade Monofamba made a laconic memorable speech under the banner; **FOR THE LIBERATION OF THE FATHERLAND.**

'Every enemy shall be destroyed....'No one amongst you shall either directly or indirectly betray the other. This is the only secret of our success.

'Each one is to execute his role as if he were a lone general on whose shoulder lays the total liberation of our Fatherland,

Fakulum. This is the highest mark of dedication, nationalism, patriotism, selflessness and total commitment to the noble and historic mission – The Liberation of the Fatherland.

'We liberate to emancipate and to enthrone social justice and equity. Therefore no one shall for the sake of self-glory destroy property nor shall any be so mean as to loot for self-aggrandizement. Our target is the enemy, to gain national freedom and sovereign independence, our legitimate goal guaranteed by international law. Alien rule is an international crime. It is slavery of body, soul and mind, from cradle to the grave. No people worthy of dignity surrender to such degradation.

'No one amongst you shall receive any bribe from the enemy nor enter into any secret pact with the enemy or his agent. We are fighting the people's war for the people's liberation, freedom, inherent right to justice and sovereign independence.

'Long live the Supreme will of the People
'Long live the Revolutionary Liberation Army
'Long live the National Revolutionary Redemption Party
'Long live the right to national self-determination,
'Long live the sovereign will of the people of FAKULUM'.

It was the most solemn speech ever delivered under heavens at noon. Hard things are easier handled when the hard rays of the fiery sun have been weakened by its long trek across the sky. But circumstances imposed it, more so on someone who does not defer a thing. it was a judgement than a speech. Each statement struck deep in every mind, heart and soul.

104

But Nformi Birr, the Commander of the Revolutionary Liberation Army was to come up and deliver more severe blows.

'Here today under the blazing sun and before the gods and the spirits of our fathers, stand the fighting spirit and instrumental force of our liberation. I mean you', and he thrust his finger at the men standing before him. 'The future of this nation as an indivisible unit, as a people in whose hands lie their destiny, depends fully on us and what we are prepared to do. We have a cause and we have a mission. We must not deny our children their inherent right to a befitting future in liberty, equality and dignity.'

This was received with justifiable silence of deep reflection and soul meditation. His eyes were full of rage. Every vein on his huge neck and broad face stood out distinct. He was in his military and warlike mode. Though looking fierce his voice was loud and clear.

Nformi Birr stood his full height, surveyed his men with his fiery eyes piercing every heart, then drained the sweat from his face with the left hand and continued rather poetically.

'What does one live for?
Ask yourself,
What do I live for and how do I live?
Live only to suffer and be suffered?
Live only to be exploited and deprived?
And denied the right to think and reason?
The right to analyse, discuss and judge?
The right to act according to self-conscience and interest?
The right to know what is happening in one's own country?

The right to participate in decision –making in matters
of national interest?

Has he who is denied all these?
Except the privilege to be ordered around and
instructed on,
What to do, how and when to do it;
Any mandate to call self a being?
Has he who accepts this condition conscious of
personal self-worth and dignity?
Can there be human dignity,
Without the right to natural and social justice?

He who has no right to the good things of life
Has no right to life;
Even the misery of its nature
He who is suppressed, deprived and exploited
He who is enslaved
And lives for the goodness of his oppressor
Lives not, he exists in emptiness.

He who only exists, enjoys and exercises no freedom
And he who has no freedom
Controls not his own destiny
It is the freedom to think, reason, act and choose
That gives you mastery of your destiny
And a people suffocating under foreign domination
and alien rule control not their destiny
Or who surrender to the barbarity of alien rule and
rape of their dignity
Deny themselves their rightful place in the history of
free humanity.
This has been our plight for too long!

'This has been our condition. Our forefathers fought gallantly against the white man, our slave-driver, but were betrayed. Our elders say that when fire burns you, you run away from wood-ash. Received wisdom equally admonishes that if a snake bites you, you have to be extra careful even with a millipede. But ours is more than that; it's the blacksmiths furnace out to annihilate us from the face of the earth. We are in the devil's hell fire!

'That history may not repeat itself; we have called for unity, absolute unity, and total commitment to the struggle. By naming a child Wepngong we emphasize one thing that the individual should fear, respect and abide by the collective will of the people, for there can be no world without the people. As iron sharpens iron, so in solidarity, one man sharpens another for the collective good and collective survival in dignity.

'We should all remember that an ant's hole is big enough for rain water to enter through and flood the house, thereby bringing the structure to its foundation. Indeed, if there is any time in our history when 'bong abee' 'abee yu ngir,'and 'fo ni nwe' should assume total unifying force, spiritually, morally, intellectually, and physically, it is now.

'We must either collectively and resolutely act now or we are doomed, doomed forever. Do our elders not say that the elephant's fats taste better when warm? The task before us is enormous but in solidarity we will overcome. This country; FAKULUM, Nyu Ngong made no mistake in dedicating it our eternal heritage. Thank you! Thank you' Thank you very much as you commit yourself to patriotic service.'

His words were greeted with the raising of weapons. Every heart was boiling with rage. It was as if a titled man, respected all over the kingdom, had been challenged or called a woman before his kinsmen in the market- place.

At the end of the inspiring soul-searching speeches, Tantoh Ncham Ncham carried himself solemnly to the centre and stood before two medicine pots. Inside the *pots of ngang* were different mixtures with sharp scents, the blood of a lizard, the excreta of a python, bones of a lion, a cone of black ants and a multitude of pounded fresh and dried leaves. Tied around the pot were the *rlang*, leaves of *nkeng*, and the quills of a porcupine and the bushy tail of a squirrel. The red band tying them round the pot was well soaked with the blood of the white cock sacrificed, unto the gods to lead the struggle. Unlike in normal sacrifices, neither the wine was tasted nor the cock eaten.

In between the two pots, the medicine man laid the dead cock, and by it stood a white dog. With a two edged machete pointed into the sky, he stood as if transfixed. Except for his lips that moved, his eyes, wide- opened, were focused up to the heavens and they blinked not. No sooner did he bring down the machete that lightning struck and consumed both the dog and dead cock. The ground, soaked with three calabashes of palm wine, became as dry and dusty as the soil of drought struck savannah.

'The act of the gods; so shall it be with any amongst you who goes against the will of the people and turns his back on the oath we have taken here. Remember, what chases a rat to inevitably dash into fire must be hotter than the fire itself.

The six units passed in between the two pots, with Nformi Birr leading and Tamfu Bingir taking the rare. It was the most solemn moment. In taking the oath of fidelity, each knelt down in between the pots and leaked the contents of each pot with his tongue and then the dry dust. As he did this, his weapons were slung across his shoulders and he held them with his two hands. Each in taking the solemn oath declared allowed, 'If I betray the people my sins shall find me out.'

'Mark you,' called Tantoh Ncham Ncham who had stood watching the oath taking, 'treachery is an abomination and has no cure,' and he moved out solemnly, neither speaking to any nor looking back.

Chapter Twelve

Three nights to the fateful day, Nformi Birr with his magic and sorcery- filled body, transformed himself into a kite and flew to Mbarere, the Capital City which was under the command of his second in command. Well briefed of the preparations, and satisfied with what he saw, he was ready for the next step. He removed his *'nsip mnchep'* (small gourd of medicine) shook it three times tipped some quantity on his left palm and leaked it.

'Cross your hands,' he instructed Tamfu Bingir. On each palm he tipped a pinch which Tamfu licked beginning with the right. With a gentle tap on the shoulder, his lieutenant was winged and they flew all over Mbarere sprinkling the *'njie'*. This was a very powerful mixture of leaves and water brought from Nyamngai.

The **njie**, an incomprehensible mixture, had two functions. One, it made men sleep like drunken women. Second, the charm, even in the full glare of the sun, casts dark clouds before the enemy, making escape difficult and ability to see and attack their assailant impossible.

Back in Ladouma, the headquarters of the Revolutionary Liberation Army, he rounded up his assignment. In one instance, he transformed himself into red ants, in another into a chameleon, yet in another instance into a **chorung**. Through these means, he applied his **njie** all over Ladouma, most especially in the GRAs, within the army, gendarmerie and police headquarters.

In the heart of Ladouma, as in Mbarere, he buried the pot of **ngang** as instructed by the medicine- man.

At the agreed time on that Sunday morning at the first cock crow, the six provincial headquarters had their baptism of fire.

Mbarere and Ladouma were awakened to an eruption of surprise attack. The red-capped men, guarding important buildings and lords, were silenced to eternal sleep from the temporary. Two prison yards, one in each town in which political detainees found their hell on earth, were captured; all guards rewarded retributively and the inmates liberated. They had a twilight of hope they had been promised and they joined the ranks of the liberation army.

The stench of blood, roasted property of animates and inanimates filled the air. Confusion and the bell of death rang into every ear as the men of the GRAs, the guarded who enjoyed their heaven on earth, awakened by the air filled wailing, stinking smell of roasted flesh and property, discovered that their helmeted and red- berated guards armed to the teeth, had long since been silenced to eternal slumber.

In Ladouma where the operations were under the direct command of Ta Nformi Birr, the greatest success was recorded. The early morning air was abnormal as it was filled with the groans and wails of the wounded and the dying. Those with hearts and minds still alert, who sprang to their feet for an escape, went no further than the door. Some, too shocked to respond to the dictates of the circumstances, stood motionless and helpless and could only be rewarded in kind. Ta Nformi Birr's single slash of his razor-blade sharpened machete opened up the belly of the Commander of the Gendarmerie and the content therein poured down messily. With the strands of the hair in the grip of his fingers, the huge head was neatly sliced off.

From the next house emerged the Director of Maritime Trade who himself had many plantations, shops and houses, trying sleepily to escape. With this razor-blade sharpened machete, Nformi Birr had his head opened up from top to the neck. Others, of no choice of theirs, had their routes to eternity in the infernos that engulfed the glorious mansions of yesterday's elect.

In Ladouma alone, twenty-five whites lost their lives. The black-white men casualty was very high, and as for property damage, no accurate estimate could be made.

Reports from Mbarere and other provincial headquarters recorded great successes too. The grand success in Ladouma in particular and the release of many prisoners as well as the capture of ammunition from the garrisons was an inspiration which signaled the fall of colonial misrule.

As the communication links were the first to neatly suffer disconnect, each of the six provincial capitals was isolated and it took time before the Governor General was brought into full knowledge. To have the situation under full control, a state of emergency was proclaimed and a full scale war was declared on the nationalists who were now brandished terrorists,' 'communists,' 'agents of anti-civilization, democracy and Christianity.'

Monofamba, Honourable Bongbih and Ta Nformi Birr were declared wanted and a heavy cash reward awaited anyone who had word of their whereabouts or could produce them, dead or alive. The nationalist movement and the 'National Revolutionary Redemption Party (NRRP) was banned and any found in possession of their literature or suspected of having links with the movement was arrested, tortured and beheaded and head displayed at strategic, cross roads for all to see. This was the gruesome barbarity used to dissuade natives from joining the NRRP for their political salvation and counter strategy to annihilate the struggle for independence.

In having the barbarian fight the barbarian, the first troops sent into the forests of Mbarere and Ladouma and other important towns were the natives, trained for columns of the Colonial Frontier Force, (CFF). In Ladouma and Mbarere with

Nformi Birr and Tamfu Bingir still applying the *njie* charm, three days passed and not even a soul came back to tell the tale.

It was now evident that more serious steps had to be taken. The Governor General, in a desperate move, applied for special military reinforcement and ammunitions from HOME. Plane loads of arms and men were air- lifted. With this reinforcement, Ladouma the stronghold of the Liberation Army, was first invaded with planes hawking above, dropping paratroopers here and there.

Applying the **njie** charm, Ta Nformi Birr and his men fought gallantly for three days without a break. As the enemy found it hard to pierce through the dark clouds in order to shoot at the assailant; those of the Liberation Army who fell, were caught by accidental bullets. In triumph, they mowed down enemy after enemy. The fallen were so many that none of the victors gave a damn to the severing of heads any more. But not so with the whites whose heads commanded special place of honour. The paratroopers were much to be pitied as many landed down with poisonous spears stuck either into the anus or with the intestines gushing out and tongues hanging pitiably.

As if to give General Pierre an opportunity to try his luck, Ta Nformi Birr was face to face with him at close range. The General, grimacing, had his revolver pointed at the centre of his forehead and fired. The bullet caught him at the exact target for he was a seasoned soldier that had fought the Germans in their two wars and the Vietnamese. From the sound it was evident the bullet had hit but a hard solid metal. Indeed fire sparked and the bullet dropped miserably on the ground.

Enraged beyond limit after the third bullet had dropped same, he charged like a wounded lion with his bayonet. Ta Nformi Birr stood without moving. At close range and with all his might and skill, he drove the bayonet within the region of the heart to split it into two and thereafter to gallantly put his left foot on the barbarian's head. The sharp-pointed bayonet struck but a hard rock and twisted.

Ta Nformi Birr held him by the throat with his left hand and looked at him straight in the blue-eyes turning red. 'You, agent of our dehumanisation, yesterday was your day, today is mine.' The man was chocking, his legs trembling below so violently. He struck him on the head with the **rlang** in his right hand three times and the man gave a throaty cry, turned round and round as if in a tornado and collapsed miserably. As he collapsed he passed out and a stench smell filled the air. His lieutenants who were with him unable to withstand fled for their life. With this unprecedented masculine victory Ta Nformi Birr eulogised triumphantly **'Nsi Mbete!' 'Nsi Mbete!!' 'Nsi Mbete!!!'**

The *Mbeh* answered triumphantly 'Hmmm! Hmmm! Hmmm! Hmmm! Hmmm!' The natives in the colonial army understood the meaning and advised their masters. The retreating enemy, in great confusion and disarray, were chased in jubilant shouts of triumph and mowed down here and there. The colonial over- lords listened to the sad tale with incredulity as those who managed to escape related it. The coloniser's backbone was definitely broken when it was discovered that General Pierre had been captured and slain like a sacrificial lamb.

This defeat tasted so bitter and revolting to the colonial mind. It was worse than the defeat the colonial master had suffered at the hand of Hitler or in Vietnam.

In the Colonial Security Council, chaired by the Governor General, it was agreed that direct fighting would not break the spine of the Liberation Army so long as the leader was invulnerable to whistling bullets.

'Your Excellency, I have been in black Africa for too long,' observed the Secretary General to the Governor General. 'Black magic coupled with sorcery and witchcraft, as we are subjected to, can't be overcome by any means other than treachery. I should remind you that the occupation of this territory gave our metropolitan government the greatest headache and humiliation. Learning from history and more so realising that this same baboon of a human species is the direct descendant of the man at whose hands we were dragged in the mud in this African jungle we must change tactics. We should send a monkey to catch a monkey.'

Chapter Thirteen

Ta Nformi Birr, on the third month after the triumphant victory, felt extremely weak. He went to bed earlier than usual. No sooner did he fall on his mat than he was drawn into a deep sleep. The sweet sleep was soon over taken by a spirit-tormenting dream. In his dreamy world, Ta Nformi Birr saw himself carrying a pot of delicious meat and bottle of beer in hand. From the sky descended three hawks with long beaks and claws. In a single swoop and within the blink of an eye, the pot was emptied by these avaricious creatures. This grand success seemed to have maddened the winged beasts, and in triumph they came back for his eyes, ears, tongue and head.

Bewildered by the behaviour of these wild creatures of the sky, he reached out for his staff to crack their heads open, but it was not there. He tried to reach out for his machete, spear or any weapon at all, there was none handy. Grieved to heart he threw the bottle of beer at them caught none. He then turned to face the wild creatures with his hands. Employing both hands and feet, he fought hard but the harder he struck, the more they were strengthened and determined to have him as their prey. The more he kicked, not even a feather dropped down. He was bewildered. But being a man of action, surrender to these wild creatures was not a thing to be contemplated.

With his whole body on heat, as if on fire, his head pulsating with pain from the pecking of the wild creatures, he stretched his hand for the three tied elephant stalks, inherited from his father Tata Ngoh, and the '*rlang*'. Behold they were gone. In frantic confusion, he tried to escape for his dear life but his feet could carry him nowhere. It was his shout for help that woke him up. There, outside his hut, in the dull peeled early morning light, he could see dimly three strange fellows. The successful hunter had been trapped in the cool morning air of the day. In disbelief, he crouched down as if preparing for a frog jump, wiped his eyes with his two hands to awaken himself to the numbing reality before him.

Betrayed and now trapped like a caged rat, he tried hard to recite any of his powerful potent words, those that transform him either into ants, a kite or a chameleon, but no success. But he knew even a caged rat still has the spiritual will power to rebel and fight back for self-survival. Conscious of this survival instinct in all living things and that which is higher in man, he then stretched his hand for the *nsip mnchep* in which was the *njie* charm, but his hand was mortified as his eyes fell on Tamfu Bingir.

Death ghastly stared him in the face. His lungs and his head were all on fire. Sweat of blood poured down from his face like water. In spite of the cold morning air, he sweated even between his buttocks. But he refused to bow. Such an act will not only be treacherous, it will give the enemy and traitor a victory they do not deserve.

Before Ta Nformi Birr, grinning triumphantly was Lt. General Jacque Blande who took over from General Pierre with the *rlang* raised up in victory. It was this that enabled them to overcome the already cast *njie* charm. Behind him was Tamfu Bingir the commander of the Mbarere Revolutionary Liberation Army Unit carrying the three tied elephant stocks! Taking the rare was another white soldier carrying the exhumed medicine pot. This was responsible for Ta Nformi Birr's inability to apply the *njie* charm again. His seeing the source of their age- long supernatural powers in white hands, grieved him more than the certainty of his betrayal and imminent death.

'It is not I that am betrayed, but our people; the people's will and survival in dignity; for I am only an individual. It is the future of our children and generations yet unborn. As for me,' he thought to himself, 'I am only a symbol of my people's will and an instrument for the attainment of legitimate aspirations and freedom through national sovereignty.'

Then he turned sharply and addressed the traitor, 'And you, Bingir, know that what you have done isn't against Ta Nformi Birr. It is against us all, including your own children and your children's children. Where, on earth, have you ever heard of a titled man betraying his people? Where on earth have you ever heard of a man, successor to his father's Stool in no less an institution than the Nfuh collaborating with the people's enemy for crumbs from under the table? Where in living memory have you heard of a titled man selling his father's and grandfather's graves? No one, not even the worst debtor sells the family kola-nut tree. But here you have sold both the living and the dead for nothing more than the crumbs that will fall from your white master's table. But remember the oath! The oath, the oath we sore! Remember my father's dying words...Mind you, the chicks of the hen that go loitering with the chicks of the hawk will sooner than later become soup for the latter. And for you, colonial master, you may dream of victory, but your victory will last only for a season... I will die but the spirit and will of the people for freedom, truth; justice and dignity will not be dead. There is no giving up! WE WILL NOT SURRENDER!'

This so much provoked Lt. General Blande's patience that he gave him a hard slap. 'Shut up! How dare you say that? How dare you have the guts to say such nasty things to me? You beast! Your life is in my hands,' and he slapped again, 'bga-a' 'bga-a' and Ta Nformi Birr spat blood from his mouth into his blazing eyes. And it pained like real tropical hot powdery pepper. The General screamed in awful pain wriggling his hand which had gone numb from slapping Ta Nformi Birr.

'I don't blame you. I have no time with you, a devil. Where it not for this traitor, where would you have seen me before slapping and calling me 'beast'? Our elders say that unless the wind blows you cannot see the anus of a fowl. Do what pleases you but the truth is written in gold on the rocks of this land.

'One last word for you and he who has handed me over to you, may it please you to know that 'The sun that sets shall rise and that every rising sun is brighter and more inviting and promising than the sun that set!'

The words stung Tamfu Bingir and he wept bitterly and repentantly. But it was too little, too late.

And Lt. General Blande who was in serious pains ordered his men to treat him like a beast that deserves no respect. But he, Lt. General Blande, never recovered his eye sight in spite of expert treatment he received HOME.

Tamfu Bingir as Commander of the Revolutionary Liberation Army in Mbarere, the capital city, was lured to betray the people's hope and champion of freedom. Like Judas Iscariot who was singled out by the enemy to betray the Saviour of the universe, Tamfu Bingir, the closest to the commander of the people's liberation army was used to reveal the source of the invincibility of the people's liberation army. Lured with beer, wines and spirits and rich delicious foods he got drunk. And like Samson in the hands of Delilah, the beautiful fleshy damsels drilled to charm him and under the influence of alcohol, Tamfu Bingir leaked out the time honoured secrets.

Three days before the sad news reached Nyamngong and most specifically Ntooh, HRH the Nyamndom had a real disturbingly sleepless night. He woke up and went out quite early in the morning, if such a change would calm his nerves and give him peace of mind. Above him, he saw a pale moon in the sky. This was too unusual, whenever the sky was blue and clear. Still lost in his thoughts, his dog gave its 'woof – woof' bark and got away to a distance for safety. But this was his own dog that had always been under the throne and running up to him and waxing the tail whenever it saw him. But here, Kaplar, the royal dog dashed away from HRH the Nyamndom for the first time since it became a familiar face whenever HRH was seen either in private or public. This new development was most disturbing. Added to the dream, it was more than an entertainment joke. It raised the stakes even far higher and HRH's nerves stood on end.

'What is amiss? What an omen!' HRH queried shaking his head heavily. And cold shiver descended on HRH and he tried in vain to shake it off.

But Kaplar, would have had a peace of mind if it could unload the burden it had on. Though scared of HRH it could not talk. It was ill at ease. In deep reflection, HRH recalled the fable that in the beginning dogs used to talk. And that they were wise and had double eyes and interested in saving the lives of the innocent from the vicious mischiefs of the wizards and witches, the dog would report the evil doers to the elders for necessary action to save life. Angered by the dog's activities that exposed them thus endangering their own lives, the wizards and witches ganged up and blocked the dog's power of speech. Man then lost a guaranteed source of information to save life though the dog has remained man's greatest companion since creation.

This rather than give relief added greater pain and psychological torment to HRH.

When it was day dawn, Kwimnchep complained to the mother-in-law that she spent the whole night battling with one dreadful dream after the other.

'Unable to have a wink without a nightmare, I stood up and made a fire---- But no sooner did I finish than I started sleeping on the chair and the bad dreams followed me. Mama,' she addressed her mother-in-law, 'I fought with the dreadful dreams till day- dawn came as a big relieve. I have never had this experience......Tell them Mama' (referring to her father-in-law) 'for this cannot be for nothing,' she insisted wearing a heavily grave face.

The mother-in-law listened to this pathetic story, shook her head sadly and heaved a big sigh.

'My daughter-in-law, I will', she said with her left hand supporting her head.

That same morning, while taking her usual solid breakfast made up of overnight corn fofoo and warmed green vegetable, her mind wondered far and wide. A cold shiver ran through her spine and it showed on her face. This gave her a bitter taste in her mouth and her mouth went 'dead' for the food. Thoughtlessly, she flung away the pot of soup which she had held in her left palm, thinking it was the ball of fofoo for which she had no appetite any more. It was the shattering sound as the soup pot landed on the ground outside on the court yard that led the grand daughter to shout, 'Ah Mama you have thrown the soup- pot outside. See, it is all reduced into small pieces', she lamented.

Mama rose up her face gravely; and on seeing the splintered pieces and the remaining quantity of vegetable retired to bed weakly, without a word, turning her back on the inmates and the world in painful resignation. This was unusual, for the sun, her usual companion after fire, was just rising, heating the cold air outside.

The two nights that followed were no better, if not worse. All over Nyamngong, sorrow gripped everyone. No one knew why, except those with double eyes who saw it and concealed it until when, like eighth month-old pregnancy, it could no longer be concealed.

On the second night, a pestilential owl, in its hooting, instilled fear and horror in every heart in Ntooh. As if this was child's play, *'gfung'* the witch bird, gave out its foreboding shrill cry 'via-arr'. Immediately the shrill sound died down, two more opened their devilish beaks from opposite ends of Ntooh. The game plan gave the impression of designed competition between the *bgfung* (witch birds). It was no doubt some planned act of terror visited on the people, two owls then took over, but this time with some modification. The owl with a shallow voice tuned while the other with a baritone crooking voice answered. This went on with periodic breaks, as if for refueling, far into the early morning hours of the day.

The next day, HRH the Nyamndom summoned his men with double eyes to tell him what was amiss. Indeed there was no doubt in any mind that something bad was to happen, for the past three nights were most disturbing. What he wanted to know was the nature of the imminent danger.

124

Chapter Fourteen

On receiving the heart breaking message of the father's death, Njemucharr left for home to see his widowed mother, his twice – widowed grandmother, HRH the Nyamndom and his fatherless brothers and sisters.

The journey home was nothing else but irksome. The weight of loss and the pains of sorrow were all devastatingly married on him. They were crushing. He sat all through putting up a long face. Any effort to shake him out of this stupor only imposed it the more. There was no escaping and no denying the fact that he was out of himself. This was a painful and crushing fact.

Conversations in the lorry were dominated by the conflicting stories about the anti-colonialists, now referred to by the establishment as subversive elements and communists. European colonial powers to defend their interests and justify their mindless repression of liberation forces to keep their colonies often accused nationalist movements of communism. This was the logic of the bipolar politics of the era. To the colonial powers Africans had no interests to be respected, no mind and no independent judgement of their own. They had no right to choose their friends: they had been trapped and imbued with a colonial mindset which should condition them work eternally for European interest.

The colonialists and their agents presented the liberators as enemies of the country. Every imaginable negative was associated with them. But patriots saw the death of the commander as the greatest tragedy that had ever befallen a people. As to the manner of his death, one version had it that he was burnt to death, another version maintained that his body was hued into small pieces. Njemucharr who was so terrified by the verdict of his never going to see his father was only comforted by the fact that many saw foreign rule as evil. Fortunately the roads had not yet gone bad, so there was no pushing.

It was dusk when he alighted from the lorry. He had made up his mind not to be seen by anyone before he winked at the mother. The distance he had to walk offered him an ideal opportunity to execute his plan to the letter.

From *'Rtu Lunga'* over-looking Nyamntoh, he stood and studiously surveyed the compound and his heart seemed to melt from within.

Njemucharr's mind wandered far and wide. Through his mind's eyes, he saw his mother in grief and heard her wail and mourn like a spoiled teenage girl. In trying to picture his future, he saw nothing but darkness and emptiness. Though it was not cold, he found himself shivering. He raised his eyes and looked upon the large compound with houses sprawling to the west as with many young men moving out of the already congested space to build at the gentle slope.

He longed for the sweet and inviting music of water carriers at the setting of the sun:

'Nwe mu du mba roh le?'
'Eh lee! lee!'

And, unfortunately, he heard none of such sweet sounds. He waited for the crying of babes as mothers or nurses hand them over to someone to do this or that house chore before darkness fell. But there was nothing. He could not even hear any meaningful sound. Though he listened keenly, what he got was grave silence. The deafening silence itself could not be denied, it was heavy in the air.

In his agony and pensive mode, he tried to pip into the future. The reward he had from his effort was a splitting frontal headache. It seemed his head was giving way into two. The high

126

temperature in his head made him think that hot coals from the burning furnace had been packed into his skull. He quietly lowered his small wooden box on his head, placed it on the ground and sat on it. With his head in his hands, it seemed everything around him was turning so swiftly. The ground was as well spinning and he could now only hear sharp pains inside his head. He started wondering if that was his own end.

When he finally regained some consciousness, he shook his head, the pain and heat already gone, he turned and looked upon the compound again and this time he saw the smoke of evening supper bidding the receding light farewell.

Though this smoke rose from many houses, it was thin; having risen through the grass- roofed houses quickly faded away. This in itself testified to the gravity of the grief-stricken royal-family.

Under normal circumstances, there should have been much singing, the shrill sweet voices of the young girls either balancing the water calabashes acrobatically on their heads or trying to loll the babes to sleep.

As Njemucharr sat transfixed, confused, he tried to imagine his father resurrecting and wondered whether he would be received joyously or that the grief-stricken would reject him on account of his being a ghost. In an effort to reflect on this awesome thought of his, he was startled by the ugly hooting of an old owl on a stump at no distance from him. He picked up his small wooden box and raced down the road breathlessly as fast as his legs could carry him.

It was more than three weeks since the death of Nformi Birr. Grief-stricken Nyamngong and, most especially Nyamntoh, were still buried under the heavy dark clouds of sorrow. Neither time nor the periodic rains were enough to wash away the burdensome grief hopelessness and helplessness under which they lived. Men sobbed and women wailed for the great loss. Many men concluded that the generation of great men was past.

But men develop great potentialities as they positively exploit given opportunities for their common. The more they sit in conference and discuss issues freely, the more they compete, such sharpen and enrich skills and ideas. But now the gathering of people for whatever purpose was banned. Men were not allowed to move about with any kind of weapon, not even their traditional sheath machete and spears; things which in all Nyamngong were regarded as a mark of maturity and masculinity. The *Mndap Ngwa*, social institutions which served as traditional banking systems, could no longer hold, under the emergency laws. It was as if life had been nailed to the cross.

Though religious gatherings were not proscribed, they were confined to their buildings: churches and mosques; no public preaching and processions of any kind were allowed. Sermons were monitored and nothing negative about the imperial government was tolerated. However positive issues as the abolition of cannibalism, the protection of twins, abolition of slave trade, abolition of inter-tribal wars were highlighted, giving room for peace, stability and development, but above all the introduction of western education, building of churches and other innovations brought on the wings of capitalist expansionism. This was the strategy to divert attention from the multiple evils of colonial rule has imposed reducing the subjugated into minions. Under the circumstances this was compounded by the operating emergency laws which have disempowered people, men, women, and children no exception.

The Nyamngong received these sermons in discontent, for they knew nothing about cannibalism and twins, referred to as '*Bo Nyu*' were highly honoured. As regards the abolition of inter-tribal wars and slave trade the Nyamngong shuddered at this, for how could a medicine man pride on having cured a wound on the finger by driving a sword through the patient's heart?

In this colonial drive, two themes became favourite frequently dosed out in all churches. These were 'turning the other check', instead of retaliating and not 'laying one's treasures on earth where moth and mice will destroy'. These were capitalist sermons, which like opium, dosed the victims to their graves, for naked exploitation by the coloniser, Njemucharr understood this after a careful analysis.

Chapter Fifteen

T a Nformi Birr was a man whose death celebration could have been superseded only by his father's. He should have been buried with full military honours, with women behind closed doors. Men should have come out in their military outfits to demonstrate how they would have fought to defend and save him, if it were the question of valour. War trumpets should have blended the numerous war songs and those who had brought skulls home should have displayed their skulls. And of course those he brought home himself, in addition to his father's, should have been exhibited. Rather than mourning and wailing in ashes, it should have been the celebration of the life of a great man, a hero.

But under the circumstances, there was no beating of the mother drum to produce its bellowing sound. There was no firing of the guns which should have begun with the lowering of the remains into the grave. The *'Nya-Nfu*,' with its frightening roaring 'Vuum! Vuum!! Vuum!!!' Hmm! Hmm!!' sound, which should have awakened all the Nyamndoms, Tatah Ngoh and all other great men gone before, to await the arrival of their great son, was not heard.

The murder of Ta Nformi Birr was an irreparable loss, but must painfully; it was made to look like the death of a mad dog. It was a tragedy, a calamity unequal in the history of man. Men, even titled men, sat mournfully akin to peacocks whose wings have been drenched in red palm oil. This was the handiwork of treachery, as such the Nyamngong regard treachery as the worst abomination.

In the death of a man of Ta Nformi Birr's status, the gathering of people, men coming and firing guns, in-laws bringing goats and other prescribed rites, the different Jujus and all kinds of dances from different parts of the kingdom, remove the loneliness and minimise the weight of grief in the relations. In fact in Nyamngong you can safely prejudge the status of the dead from the rites performed; the Jujus at the celebration, the duration and the composition of and population at the celebration.

The circumstances of Ta Nformi Birr's death and the aftermath made the wife, most especially, weep that her husband had been killed like a mad dog and left on a shrub for the birds of the air. HRH the Nyamndom, refused to taste anything for three days, for to him, his tongue had been removed from the mouth. Ma Ndabu, the mother who had lost her husband Tatah Ngoh in the same manner, wept and lost her power of speech. Her eyes grew swollen and ember red. After the death of her husband, Ta Nformi Birr whom she addressed, 'my husband', was her only hope of sustenance. She now called herself 'the twice-widowed woman who ever lived'.

To the Nyamngong death is not the end of human life. It is a transition, a journey to meet those gone before. When they weep, it is like saying good bye to a loved one leaving on a long journey of no return. Mourners solemnly sing "Go softly! Go softly! Let your road be straight and smooth!'

In all respects, Njemucharr bore the brunt of the sufferings, the pains of grieve and loss, all married into one. The weight was crushing but he could transfer it to no other person.

When Njemucharr entered the house unexpectedly, there were renewed wailing cries. His grandmother who was just about sleeping off was awakened by the shrill cries. On seeing Njemucharr standing and sobbing in depression, she stretched out her arms in visible helplessness, and Njemucharr came in, weeping and trembling.

Behind, his mother tried to stand up from among other women but sauntered and collapsed with a chucking cry in her throat. Njemucharr, fearing that calamity was happening, turned sharply to assure himself of the mother's safety. He helped her to her feet and led her back to the mat on the floor, where there were scores of mourning women.

Three weeks of continuous weeping, of agony, and of psychic be-numbness, had reduced his grandmother into a skeletal frame with the flesh sticking out so loosely. The face, the toothless mouth, now fully exposed her sunken jaws and disproportionately bulging eyes. She wept, 'Oh my husband, when you were alive, you were my own world. I could not exchange the world with you. I knew you were to bury me like a Queen. But now you are no more. When I die the hawks would feast on this old carcass!'

In all sincerity she tried to spill what was left of her store of tears. At first she only wetted the strained eye- lids. As if reminded by her sub conscience that one never mourns one's own death, she pressed hard and a bulb dropped miserably. Assured by the misery of the hard earned drop, she stopped for any further pressing, would only have illuminated the dryness of the eyes.

As for Kwimnchep who sat in the dark, and wailed in agony, it was a deluge. The flow was torrential as if nature in his omniscience and mercy supplied her with more tears than necessary for any single woman. If shedding of tears and self – infliction of punishment could appease the gods to send back the dead to life, Ta Nformir Birr should have been the first. If there had ever been a woman who ever felt and practically demonstrated the grievous loss of her husband, Kwimnchep had no rival.

'Kwimnchep be mindful. Know that too much weeping disturbs his smooth journey to meet the ancestors' a sympathiser admonished her.

Others, in reminding her of the fertility of her womb, admonished: 'You are sitting here naked soothing your jaws that your husband is gone? You have husbands not just one husband,' referring to her five sons. 'A woman whose womb is warm and blessed of men- folk is never a widow.'

A story was told of a Ndatamabeb woman whose husband had died. But when the corpse was taken from the house for burial, she insisted that she be buried with her bosom husband. She held up the burial ceremony for more than two hours. When people lost their patience they stopped holding her.

'Leave her. I am ready with burial ground to cover her once she falls in' screamed one of the young grave diggers. But instead of jumping into the grave, she jumped over and with her hippopotamus size and weight pushed weak observers who stood in her way flat to the ground.

Both sympathisers and onlookers, burst out laughing as she quietly retired to her house without waiting to perform the eternal farewell by throwing some soil on the corpse wrapped in cloth and laid on a mat in the grave. But many who saw Kwimnchep concluded that if the husband were not buried far away in the bush by the enemy, she would have surprised people with one calamity or the other.

When Njemucharr saw his mother, she was all skeleton, a shadow of her former self, she who had been a bulky, beautiful tall woman, fair in complexion. In her youth, she was the talk of the kingdom. With an elegant built it was as if god had spent more time on molding her than he did on other women of her generation. She was a perfect example of nature's beauty.

Though many young men demanded her hand in marriage, but when it became clear that she was betrothed to Ta Nformi

Birr, many enviously wondered if such a perfect pair would live together to blessed old age.

Ta Nformi Birr himself was tall, strongly built with a broad hairy chest, fair in complexion and very handsome. In addition to these gifts, it was said that right from youth his back had never lain flat on the ground. He began being trained as an army general when still very young, because HRH the Nyamndom spotted the driving force and courage of a lion in him. In all respects he was a man whom any girl could have given in anything to become his wife.

After seven days of mourning and restlessness with his family, Njemucharr came to understand that his father's death had grave consequences for him. First and foremost he was the first born of his father and a boy; following him were four boys and two girls of his mother plus two other children of his father's second wife.

In addition to these there was his partially blind grandmother plus his two mothers. The mantle of great responsibilities descended on him and he could feel the weight. Outside his family responsibilities was his determination to complete his education, for as his father told him, the white man was ruling the world because of his knowledge.

'My son,' he would call, 'your grandfathers and others before him became great men and are remembered for their valour, but the great men of tomorrow shall be men who have conquered and understood the white man's secrets and witchcraft. My mother's father and my father were great men who, on special occasions, drank their wine out of skulls of human beings. In fact your grandfather used to drink out of the skull of a white man. He was the first black man in the entire known world to kill a white man whom many thought impenetrable by our spears. Both the big *'njo'* with its multiple spikes that dealt the white man a death-blow and the skull are specially preserved in the palace for posterity.'

As if to be sure Njemucharr understood all that he said and implication, he would ask, 'Njemucharr, do you get me? Do you want to be a great man in future?'

'Yes papa' he would answer.

'Then do not play with your book,' he would insist. 'But know that the knowledge which you acquire must be used for the good of our country. Your grandfather died for the sake of our country and you must not bring dishonour to our name,' he warned. Njemucharr remembered all these and even more.

Throughout the holidays Njemucharr became as busy as an ant. He cut a lot of wood to make sure there was enough for his two mothers while he was away at college. With this sense of sensibility and responsibility in the young lad, light started growing in the darkness of the women's souls. Njemucharr understood that he was not only to mold his own destiny; he was to begin shaping that of others as well. The task ahead was enormous, but though at the material time he could only imagine, he was however determined to shoulder his responsibilities and do everything faithfully and dutifully.

Chapter Sixteen

Njemucharr returned to college with a new spirit and new consciousness. The imposition of the state of emergency and the unbearable atrocities that ensued to enforce the state of emergency left everyone wondering if there was anything like hell far more devastating than what descended on the people and their country. It was as if the dehumanisation under colonial rule was not enough, so the state of emergency was salt rubbed mercilessly onto a fresh-bleeding injury.

Men, youths, individually and in small groups in their created privacy, agreed that this was beyond pardon and human endurance and that resignation to fate was treacherous, an abomination. In deep reflection they came to the conclusion that acting like the cunning and resourceful hunting dog which understudies the tactics of the intelligent animal determined not to be a prey was the only logical means of regaining freedom and living in dignity. The lessons of the past were reviewed and analysed in detail. The conclusion was the urgency of new strategies and decisive action.

The people were caged in a painful reality. They lived in captivity on their own-God-given land under over bearing and insensitive foreign rulers. They did not only lose Ta Nformi Birr, the man who saw his self-worth in the greatness of his people, the imposed state of emergency, forced the people to sacrifice their identity, culture, history and dignity the more. With the proclaimed self-government with black men imbued with white-washed consciences, evil entered deep inside the house. The enemy now had a double face; black-white, white-black. Seeking to survive at all cost the stooges peddled to the exalted white thrones took the dictates from their mentors hoke, line, and sinker and with intensified repression, the masters had a free hand to effect naked exploitation and looting.

Failing to annihilate the nationalist liberation movement, the colonial lords peddled spineless men with weak knees and sweet teeth unto the colonial- thrones and withdrew to the back- ground. The black-white men were mechanical men operated from behind, by an invisible huge hand with long hawk-like claws. This weakened the movement the more especially as treachery, and blackmail were intensified. As the oppressive knot was screwed the more, freedom for which Ta Nformi Birr gave his life receded like the fading sun in the west. But the yearning in the masses for freedom was still burning unquenchably in their hearts.

Restrictions on freedom of speech, movement, assembly, thanks to survival instinct which cannot endure without self and collective expression forced men, women, and youths to individually or in small groups retire into the forest, river banks, streams to fetch water or to waterfalls where they used the natural habitat to examine their fate, sing, dance, and shout at roof tops to nourish their souls. Man, created in the image and likeness of his Creator, without self-expression is no being, but a mere robot. This withdrawal for self-expression and moral and intellectual edification was done as often as possible to hear the humanity, to reaffirm self and group identity and above all the Nyamngong identity.

The state of emergency had such a corroding effect on the physical body, the soul, the mind that if not countered in all force could reduce the man into a robot and a toy. It was agreed that mechanical manipulation of the people was the last straw to break the camel's back and annihilate their country from the map of Africa and forever assimilate the people. You cannot talk of a people without their land, their heritage, their culture, their history and you cannot talk of a country without the people. Rejecting extinction, the people resolved that this evil must be fought back and destroyed to restore their identity and dignity.

Back in the college the Friendship Social Club which Njemucharr, Berinyuy, Atem and Ndeh had founded was enhanced. The Friendship Social Club was renowned for its entertainment, drama, debates, jokes and staging of concerts in music and dance. It attracted members from all over Nyamngong and beyond and whenever it was on stage during the monthly social evenings, both college staff, and their family members and entire student body made it a date. Njemucharr though still the spiritual mentor, tactfully lobbied for Njoh to be elected the Club's President with Atem and Berinyuy maintaining their respective posts as Vice President and Secretary General. The executive of this darling club was tactfully enlarged to cover students from across the territory, male and female. To their credit the college was run by missionaries with few Africans on the staff. With the college enjoying full confidence of the colonial regime thanks to its great emphasis on Christian education, ethics and discipline, Njemucharr was well shielded to carry out his mission.

During the Easter break the leadership of the Club went on a Moral and Spiritual Retreat and Fasting (MSRF). Their choice of venue was Nyamngai. The choice of venue was not only solemn; it was historic as far as the Nyamngong are concerned, morally enriching, spiritually nourishing, culturally and historically encapsulating and intellectually inspiring. MSRF itself was a fitting shield well chosen for the season.

In this solemn environment after explaining the purpose of MSRF, he addressed his comrades from his heart.

'To talk on issues, serious issues that have banished a people into the abyss of servitude we do not need the halls as the colonialists do. We are all children of farmers, born and bred in villages and on farms. We must never forget who we are, from where we come, if we are determined to be agents of worthy change for our people and country.

'After, having been reduced to the wretched of the land we have none. Circumstances demand that we retire to Nature's glorious garden of beauty. Here we are encouraged and entertained not just by nature's beauty and serenity; above all, we are nourished and emboldened by Truth, infinite Truth. Christianity teaches us that Adam and Eve were created and lived in splendour in the Garden of Eden, with everything at their command. But when they disobeyed God's will, they lost God's favour and were chased out of the Garden. We are here in Nature's beauty and serenity to seek his good will to reclaim what he freely gave to Fakulum but an invader has confiscated. In listening to the sweet music of the birds in the woods, in watching them fly freely in the sky, flap and stretch out their wings as if to inhale more of nature's energy unperturbed....'

As if to confirm Njemucharr's analogy, swam of birds in splendid whiteness flew over their heads and landed on Merri sand-dom. Serving as the messengers of the god of Merri, these birds when in action convey important messages to the elders and the sages of the land. Their exercise of freedom and joy was spectacular and Njemucharr and his colleagues could not fail to watch in amazement.

'Comrades what we have seen is a compelling lesson for us all. Here listening to the numerous chips of insects in the bushes and watching even the different kinds of trees and their branches and the varied grasses swerve from one direction to the other as the wind blow on, we come to understand the Creator more and what he in his infinite wisdom intended freedom to human kind to be. As the giant tree has the right to grow according to nature's will, so must the shrub, the twigs

140

and the grasses. And the freedom and serenity with which they cohabit and grow adds to nature's beauty and harmony in variety. Here, each according to its kind and nature enjoys and exercises its freedom in its own right as ordained by the nature's god. The Creator, no doubt, meant the enjoyment and exercise of freedom on a higher scale for man created in his image and likeness than the animals, birds, fishes and plants. Freedom enhances human dignity and without it man is like a lifeless fish dumped on the hot sands of the desert. God in his infinite wisdom did not only create man free and equal, as a just God, he gave to each people their own inheritance. Man as God's representative on earth was to be the master, to rule and properly manage God's creation in this physical world. Man, God commanded, was to multiply, replenish and dominate the earth and not be dominated by another. This was to be done in freedom. But how can he multiply and replenish when he, like a miserable caged rat, lives in agony and mournful captivity?

'The right to express one's self freely, to move and associate with those you love and share common aspirations, to form common associations to promote accepted ideals and interests should be like the freedom we see birds and even ants exercise and enjoy as endowed for their good by nature. This is what accounts for and promotes human equality and dignity. Any restriction for whatever purpose is a violation of divine law and nature's rhythm and harmony. As the violator stands condemned, so is it with the collaborator. This evil act is a direct invitation to rebellion. Such rebellion is in defence of the will of the Supreme Being who, for his glory, created all men free and equal. You may call this legitimate and righteous rebellion if you care, for it is to restore nature's order, beauty, harmony for human excellence and for the glory of the Creator and the Merciful.

'Colonialism which instituted foreign domination and alien rule against the will of the subjugated is a brazen display of human degradation and cultural dislocation. To sustain its rule and pillage of the conquered land, colonial rule rips apart the fibres of unity through repression, policy of divide and rule, corruption, patronage and assimilation. The consequences of colonial rule, physically, economically, socially, culturally, mentally and spiritually are enormous. Colonialism has a complex legacy which to overcome must be well understood in all its ramifications. Be not deceived to see some good in foreign domination and alien rule. It is pure evil. Foreign rule and alien domination was not born out of justice, fairness and good intentions for the subjugated. It could never be. It was born out of pure avarice and indignation for other races and cultures. It is anti-divine order of things. It is anti-God, pure and simple.

'Why should some people claim superiority over others? Why should some people in addition to ruling their own country come to rule us on our land? Why should some people impose their laws, their culture on us? Why should we learn and study the history of their kings and heroes as if we have no history, no kings and no heroes of our own land? Did we complain to them that their culture, history, laws and political system is better than our own? Or did we cry to them for redemption?'

These rhetorical questions, as real as there were, caused every heart to beat faster as if they had been running for dear life from the angry fangs of a hungry lion. Anger, justified anger, rose to a crescendo against foreign domination and alien rule with its barbarity. The clouds of a bleak future became even darker and decapitating, the more the evil system persists. But Njemucharr, speaking to them from his heart, a heart that has seen it all, was not yet done with the pragmatic painting of the gory picture.

'And when we reject their kind of rule and illegal right to rule us, the result is brutality, murder, mayhem, looting and arrests and detentions in life-threatening circumstances to instil the gruesome reign of fear. If freedom is good for 'A' it is equally good for 'T' in equal measure. The right of all people to enjoy and exercise their freedom and human dignity is universal and knows neither racial nor cultural boundaries. Each people in their own rights and good conscience are better placed to know what is good for them and what is bad and they alone stand accountable to their descendants in particular, humanity in general and above all to their Creator for each action for each action they take. While positive actions, no matter how minute it may be impacts other people positively, negative and greedy actions affect others negatively. This explains why the golden role from the Master, do unto others what you prefer done unto you.

'Why should the imperialist have the audacity to corrupt the weak among us and in deception install them as the rulers against our will? These are errand boys to do the evil biddings of their mentors. And behind the mask the chains and shackles of our servitude will only be securely fastened. Indeed these are agents of imperialism. They are nothing but our task masters. They should not be trusted.

'Freedom and justice for the colonised and enslaved is never determined by the colour of the ruler, it is by the total disappearance of the chains and shackles, the bad laws, the system of economic exploitation and the end of the system of governance that instutionalised wellbeing and plenty for the few who confiscated political powers on the one hand and misery and scarcity for the many excluded from the ruler ship and participation in decision-making on the other hand. This

143

has been our lot since the advent of the white man into our land. Nothing has changed and nothing will until the reins of authority are in our hands.

Under the state of emergency in brazen disregard to our culture and history as a people, our ancestral shrines have been set ablaze, barbarism rode high throughout the land, mayhem, maiming and pogrom became an industry for the inhuman with the power of life and death confiscated in their hands as if they were the gods. Shamelessly the occupier to impose a perpetual reign of fear and crown himself with invulnerability with impunity carried out terrible acts of atrocities, with bombs reduced some villages to ashes, ripped open unarmed civilians including children and pregnant women. Youths fleeing for safety lost their limbs. Even the patients in the hospital received no sympathy. In the face of these gruesome impunities when an occupier declares open war on the subjugated under the pretext of state of emergency, we witness atrocious and bewildering silence of the UN; the world body created to defend and protect the weak and promote human freedom and dignity and international cooperation for the furtherance of world peace and democracy.

'Colonialism in theory and practice reduces the colonised to sub humanity. As a people depressed, banished to obscurity, squalor, and disenfranchised, having seen and lived the gruesome atrocities inherent in colonial rule and the high mark abusive nature of foreign domination exhibited under the state of emergency when many in our land were too mercilessly tortured to death as mad dogs; it has become self-evident that our destiny is in our hands. It is us who must rescue us from the fangs and claws of foreign rule and domination. We must count on our efforts. Our individual and collective intelligence, our collective capacity as a people with inherent right to be free and in freedom rule ourselves before looking for our friends who believe and defend human freedom and dignity and the equality of all nations, small and big as the guarantor of international cooperation and world peace based on justice.

'No angel Gabriel will come from celestial space and do it for us. Even our legend tells us that when Nyu Ngong sent Lunga, his mission was to urge our ancestors to defend themselves against an invader, be it a natural disaster or disease. Lunga did not come with heavenly bodies to fight for our ancestors. But today, the enemy is right here sitting astride over us. Are we not choking to death under his imperial weight?

'From hence the manner in which we conduct ourselves, carry on our studies, must be different from the yesteryears. Everything from religion, social studies, history, philosophy, music, science and arts must be subjected to critical analysis, must be turned inside out to determine whose interest is being served, projected and protected. Our pursuit of education should not be for the ivory tower. It should not be for self-aggrandisement nor should it be for pleasure and glory of the developed world. It should be to open our hidden talents to blossom firstly for our country and secondly for humanity in general of which we are a handsome part. We the educated elite must sink our egos, step into the shoes of the suffering masses and with transformational effect raise them out of the abyss of servitude and dehumanisation. Until we do that, we are collaborators of imperialism. Until we do that we are not safe from the explosive and just anger of those denied their place of honour, equality, dignity and decency.

Fakulum is part of the world and we are part of the community of the human race. Fakulum, like other nations, must be governed under international instruments. We are part of God's created humanity and must fully exercise and express our freedom, our humanity and enjoy the goodness of the nature of man created in the likeness of his Creator. Without his endowed freedom, man is empty; he is a caricature. Greed and the search for prestige and splendour, has divided the world, which God created wholesome, blessed and declared it good for man to enjoy, into the world of the have, who are the superior, and the have nots, who are declared inferior – the wretched of the earth by the self-proclaimed superior. We the Fakulum, by the dictate of the colonial rule belong to the latter. No one will get us out of the mess, but us.

'The cry for freedom and justice is universal. It follows the laws of nature: it is not the exclusive preserve of any race nor is it limited by religious, cultural, political, or territorial boundaries. It is the cry of humanity for greater humanity and the free and democratic nations should listen to the cries of the subjugated and dutifully lend a helping hand and not feign ignorance. To turn a deaf ear is to vote with the aggressors and the oppressors. Injustice is a global monster threatening world civilisation and justice everywhere. In our cry for freedom and justice we crave the indulgence of the free world to take judicious note of Arch Bishop Desmond Tutu's warning;`` If you are neutral in situations of injustice, you have chosen the side of the oppressor. If an elephant has his foot on the tail of a mouse and you say you are neutral, the mouse will not appreciate your neutrality.'

'And concurring with this man of God, Arch Bishop Desmond Tutu, another man of God and great crusader for human justice and equality, Martin Luther King Jnr, laments, 'History will have to record that the greatest tragedy of this period of social transition was not the strident clamour of bad people but the appalling silence of good people."

'The good people here include democratic nations and international organisations and the UN, whose mission is well defined in its Charter. The UN should know for sure that by its continuous silence it enables the lion to preside as judge over petition of the lamb against the lion's aggression, judgement in which the lion having the knife and the yam, the poor helpless lamb will never escape the death sentence by instant execution.

'The Friendship and Social Club must here and now, here by the banks of Nyamngai, here facing Merri before which rises to sublime heights, Rtu Khaa on which Lunga landed from beyond the sky and warned our ancestors of the impending invasion by Bara Mnya, define its bounding duty and mission for Fakulum. As patriots we should become the Brain Trust, Motive Force and Hope of freedom, justice, prosperity and dignity of our people. To me perpetual bondage as a captive is worse than death.

'The fight for freedom, human equality and human dignity is a task that must be done; done well, done urgently and done selflessly. We must live for a free Fakulum and better humanity as ordained by the Creator for his glory. The world cannot be free, live in peace and justice with Fakulum as part of the world in chains.

Restoring honour, justice and sanity to our land and people is an ordained obligation we the cream of our nation must faithfully and selflessly execute. Our land has been profaned and cursed by the occupier. It must first be liberated and its sons and daughters rescued from the fangs and claws of imperialism before its harmony and beauty are re-established by the Creator as he ordained and established in the spiritual realm.

'Sovereign independence will create the enabling environment for the erection of an edifice of political institutions blooming and blossoming in liberty and justice for all sons and daughters of the land. With fair and healthy competition guaranteed by the rule of law sustainable development will flourish bringing prosperity to our people and the sky will be the limit for all irrespective of social background. As the government will be the father of all, there will be no fatherless. In Fakulum sovereignty belongs to the people and those who rule serve the people.

'Thank you most sincerely, my dear compatriots. May the Almighty endow us with wisdom and lead us do his will, serve our people for his glory. Thank you. Thank you, once again.'

Njemucharr's speech was greeted with a prolonged applause and jubilation. Through his speech they saw light at the end of the tunnel. The spell of hopelessness and perpetual dependence and subjugation cast on them by colonial rule and emphasised by the state of emergency was removed and replaced by hope of victory as happened in other lands in Europe, Asia, and Latin America and even in Africa. However they all understood that as diamond cannot be polished and refined to shine without friction, Fakulum can never be free, strong and developed without the citizens making due sacrifices. They saw the sacrifices as nothing compared with the freedom and dignity to be earned 'Imperialism, colonialism has never triumphed over the will of a determined people. Nor has injustice, falsehood, imperial lies ever won a war against justice and truth and a united and determined people.' Njemucharr had concluded in his inspiring speech.

Njemucharr in his speech transformed the social club into a revolutionary council for the freedom of Fakulum. And the environment for this transformation and composition of the audience and timing of the meeting; everything fell in place as if ordained by Nyu-Ngong, the God of Love, Truth and Justice.

Njemucharr's reference to Lunga reminded his audience of the latter's mission to Nyu Ngong beyond the skies. The Nyamngong were plagued by an epidemic that claimed many lives. No house escaped the physical and mortal consequences of this strange disease. Nyamngong was attacked by an epidemic, *kintang*, a deadly disease never known in the history of Nyamngong. The death rate, of men, women and children was so rampant that the social, economic and political life was badly affected. To avoid the spread people were forced to reduce contacts with others as much as possible. It was a social stigma, not accepted and treated as a normal disease: the consequences lived with the victim even if he survived death. Those who were attacked by the strange disease suffered double for they became victims of social excommunication which was not the Nyamngong way of life.

Because there was no cure, and the efforts of renowned medicine men and magicians proved abortive, it was named *kintang- a disease brought by wizards and witches from evil spirits.* Many people died and there was the potential threat of the annihilation of the population, Lunga, the protector and mediator, took a flight into the world beyond the sky to meet Nyu Ngong. His mission was to see Nyu Ngong, who is both Creator of all things; visible and invisible, the omnipresent, omniscient and omnipotent, and plead with him how he could be silent and sit doing nothing when the people he for his glory created were being erased from the face of the earth. Lunga was determined to fervently plead for the prompt intervention of the Supreme Being and the Merciful not only to save the Nyamngong, but above all, he also believed that without the people to worship of Nyu Ngong, the great honour and glory attributed to the Supreme Being who lives beyond the reach of man will cease to be. Lunga also believed that Nyu Ngong did not create man to die but to live and worship him and his duty as protector and mediator was to draw Nyu Ngong's attention to any strange and unacceptable development for necessary action and permanent solution.

Conscious of his ordained duty as mediator and intercessor between Nyu Ngong and man, Lunga set on his mission to beyond the sky. He flew, flew and flew. Though the distance was so long, the burden on his heart made the enormous distance and number of days required for the journey meaningless.

When he arrived, he was well received by the minor gods, namely, Nyu Roh, Nyu Rlah, Nyu Nkfuv, Nyu Mbeng, who also controls thunder and lightning, Nyu Fuu, Nyu Kob and other heavenly attendees. Knowing that Lunga had travelled for long and should be hungry and tired, he was well entertained and advised to rest before they could listen to what prompted him to undertake such a tedious journey.

Lunga, worried about the fate of people left on earth, he was not interested in rest and relaxation. The urgency of empting the load on him was most compelling. Immediately after a good meal he reported he was ready for the meeting.

The meeting was chaired by Nyu Rlah.

'Lunga, on behalf of the Most Merciful and Supreme Being, the other gods and all other celestial beings, spirits and forces, I have the honour to welcome you, the first being from earth permitted to visit us. Believing in the importance and urgency of your mission we are all ears to hear you.'

'Thank you the spirit of the human race. I will be laconic for there is no time for empty pleasantries. My mission demands promptitude. I am on mission to meet the Supreme Being, Nyu Ngong. My people, the Nyamngong are plagued by a deadly epidemic. If the Supreme Being, the Omnipotent and Omniscient and Most Merciful doesn't intervene immediately and heal the people and the land, the Nyamngong will be wiped from the face of the earth. It is a matter for most urgent attention by the author and sustainner of life.'

The Chairman of the session, Nyu Rlah, thanked him for his eloquent and brief presentation. Apologising for absence of Nyu Ngong said; 'The Most Merciful has gone to attend a funeral.'

'What! Exclaimed a devastated Lunga. The Omnipotent and Omnipresent gone for a funeral? Death also here? Queried Lunga who was confronted with a new burden of conveying to humanity that Nyu Ngong and lesser gods are always very busy, that death also takes place in the world beyond the sky and that in addition to this world in which humans live, there are other worlds with only one Lord in charge.

'Yes! He is a caring God! However, we shall convey the message of your mission to the Most Compassionate and Most Merciful on his return. Thank you for coming, our Messenger to man on earth.'

'Thank you for the kind reception and audience. I must leave immediately.'

Nyu Ngong on return received message of the visit and the pleadings of Lunga. In responds to the pleadings and to put an end to further unexpected visits, Nyu Ngong decided to send the minor gods into the world to take care of worldly matters. The mission of Lunga was redefined. He was to teach mankind how to worship Nyu Ngong and present their problems through the various minor gods. Problems about health, fertility and expansion of the family and against sickness and death were to be presented to Nyu Rlah, about crops, food security were to be handled by Nyu Nkfuv and Nyu Mbeng, the giver of rain to nourish the crops for heavy yield. The latter was also consulted by those with powers to send thunder after defaulters. And in this you the complainant most have exhausted all pacific means and must be acting truthfully and in the fear of Nyu Ngong. So the roles of the minor gods were well defined and made known to man through Lunga. With this done, Nyu Ngong pulled away out of the reach of man and his mediator Lunga. The minor gods and Lunga exist in the spiritual realm and below the shores of the abode of the Supreme Being. The defined duties of the minor gods are to attain to human and earthly problems and men have to turn to them whenever deemed necessary. It is the minor gods who deal with the Nyu Ngong directly.

Lunga had landed on **Rtu Kaah** to warn people of the impending invasion by Bara Mnya because he did not want the people to live in ignorance and be exterminated by the invader and Nyamngong subjected to foreign rule and domination.

During the working session, among other positions adopted but held close to their hearts, Njemucharr proposed a Dance and song **Kitfu Mboo** – the medium by which aggressive sensitisation, political education and mass mobilisation was to be effectively carried out. After listening to his eloquent and comprehensive explanation, this was approved. And work on this started instantly!

Chapter Seventeen

'What are you dancing and smiling, my dear daughter? What type of dance is that? You are not dancing Mndong, are you?' inquired Ngandong who for more than five minutes stood admiring Yajeh, a seventeen year old girl who could not go to college for the parents were indigent. She had been dancing with all her soul, body and mind.

'Mama Ngange, I am not dancing Mndong. I am dancing *Kitfuv Mboo.*' Yajeh, with a sunshine lit face replied still dancing as enthusiastically as ever.

'Che-e my daughter!' exclaimed Ngandong, clapping her hands in admiration. 'This dance, *Kitfuv Mboo*, will make some of you the young ones go mad with excitement'. She expressed her surprise still watching Yajeh dancing seriously as ever.

'No, Mama Ngange, it will not make us go mad. It will make us go free. It reveals one's inner being and self-worth. It cheers the spirit and strengthens your being. It inspires and makes you believe in yourself as the equal of the other being'. Yajeh summed up confidently.

'But you have been dancing all this while without singing. I only see you dancing elegantly, beaming piquant smiles, clapping and changing from one style to another, jumping up and dancing forward and backwards' Ngandong observed admiringly.

'Mama Ngange, the music is from within, from my soul. As the music is whelming up and I dance to the rhythm, I see great opportunities, a new hope unfolding. Mama, without this dance, may be you would not have engaged me, a mere child, in this long conversation. It draws people together. It is a social magnet which makes people to reflect on the reality they live, their dehumanised status. And rather than resign to fate, commune for the right solution for there is no problem without a solution.' Yajeh said convincingly.

'Thank you my daughter. I have learnt something important from you'. Ngandong admitted, taking her hoe and basket to leave for her farm.

'Yes, Mama Ngange. By the way, Mama, help me remind your daughter, Lamini of our practice this evening'. Yajeh pleaded as she balanced the calabash of water on her head and left for their house. With the calabash of water on her head, though she stopped dancing, she was humming the **Kitfuv Mboo** music which brought light into the dark and hopeless chambers of her life.

Kitfuv Mboo born at Nyamngai was a dance in its own class. It was called the holy dance and its music, holy music.

Described as a dance of hope for all generations, it united both the old and the young, male and female in hope and faith in their self-worth. In place of complexes it emboldened most especially the young and the women. It made the daughters and sons of Nyamngong see their homeland, culture, history as second to none, to them Nyamngong was paradise on earth and centre of the universe.

Kitfuv Mboo gave birth to hope and a conscious assertiveness hitherto unknown. As a youth dance it was far more dynamic, more invigorating, more tantalising than other youth dances such as **Mbaya, Mndong, Mnkung** Masquerade dance, Samba, etc. It was imbued with a power of consciously assembling the people whenever its music, blended with its flutes, **ngem, kwa-kwar**, drums, to name but a few, sweetened the air invitingly. And whenever the people assembled to watch and dance their assertive spirits as a people were renewed. **Kitfuv Mboo** was a moral, spiritual and cultural rearmament. With this reawakening of sensibilities and unity of faith, compromise and defeat were banished.

It built in the vulnerable a new consciousness. It gave to all the twilight of hope and shattered the belief of inferiority based on race, class and colour. *Kitfuv Mboo* was christened the holy dance because it was a dance with a mission: it was redemptive. It restored people to their divinely ordained nature and, integrity. Governed by love, truth and justice, it was a counter force to the colonial policies of divide and rule which kept Nyamngong fragmented, weak and despoiled for the benefit of the colonial system. It stood as a fortress against falsehood, colonial make-belief, empty promises and slogans which like an opium dosed the subjugated to dependency-complex. These imposed complexes made men, even the elite, find solace in bars where they spent time gossiping even worse than idle lazy fleshy whores who hang about to prey on men.

Its music was known as holy music, not just because it was received from the gods of Nyamngai but because it was spiritually and morally enriching, intellectually revolutionising and inspiring, and physically empowering and redemptive. The holy music worked for mental decolonisation shedding light on the ills and injustices of colonial rule and its sustained exploitation through the lackeys imposed on the people. Meant to redeem the down trodden, it was anti-establishment. And to maintain its originality and purity and fight against pollution and dilution and more, it was sung only in Lingong.

It brought into real focus the true man endowed with divine favour and deeply sensitive and duty conscious. It challenged and encouraged men to uphold the Nyamngong ethical values, of being truthful, honest, just, responsible, sensitive, selfless, caring and patriotic. And being assertive the heroes of yesteryear were exhumed and made the living symbols of the true Nyamngong never to be a donkey for another mortal.

This new consciousness born of circumstances gave a new meaning to life and man's mission here on earth when confronted with evil. A patriot was he who loved his country, he who defends Truth and works for Justice. A patriot would hate alien rule to the core and would never compromise with those who hate Truth and work to promote injustice. A patriot stands and defends humanity. He is colour- blind. He does this to maintain his natural being and promote the will of Nyu-Ngong, the Supreme Being and the beginning and incarnation of LOVE, TRUTH and JUSTICE.

In God's infinite wisdom he created a world of diversity. He did not create a superior race and a superior culture and superior language. To abhor foreign imposed ideas that question your being and identity, that drag your integrity in the mud and action taken to reject imposition of foreign domination and alien rule, be it political, cultural, economic, religious, linguistic, historical, legal, is doing God's will and defending the Creator's wisdom of beauty in diversity. Respecting this principle and to sustain its purity, *Kitfuv Mboo*, the holy dance and holy music meant many things to different people. Its inspiration opened up to new expressions and new ways of self-expression. It was as if minds that had been folded up, held captive to rot away were loosened and creativity and inventions bloomed and blossomed.

In addition to music and styles *Kitfuv Mboo* needed new instruments. Men, women, youths, the educated and non-educated competed freely to serve their collective interests. As the mind became more inquisitive and focused, so was the hand stretched out to translate into concrete reality what the mind conceived and fashioned theoretically.

In addition to uniting the people, in the face of the odds and challenges, *Kitfuv Mboo* music dealt with reality. The older generation unfolded the true history and culture of the people, the history of their great kings and heroes. With the unknown, known, the women and youth formulated new songs extolling the great deeds and victories of the past. Inspired by such great deeds of yesteryear, the people were convinced that the lions and tigers of yesterday could never have given birth to sheep in the land. And if in the past invaders, such as the *Bara Mnya* and with exceptional guerrilla war tactics, the Hock Long Nose people from the evil world were repulsed and other challenges such the deadly *Kintang* were overcome, the present would be no impossibility. The people discarded colonial maxims which held them in humiliation as upstarts and saw themselves as doers of great things who should not be the under dogs of others.

As good palm wine never conceals itself and easily gets admirers and a good buyer, *Kitfuv Mboo,* though started in Nyamngong, soon got converts and disciples outside the land of its birth. It spread like wild fire to cover the entire national territory. In Bakwa an old dance known as *Mbanglum* was given a revolutionary touch in the likeness of *Kitfuv Mboo.* Bakwa being a transit town for recruited labourers for the plantations, *Kitfuv Mboo* was exported to the plantations. It became a national symbol of redemption of the people of Fakulum who were victims of divide and rule, repression and whose culture was being eroded and badly undermined by the state of emergency. The people's integrity and identity were like the setting sun fading in the west. The character of the people, under the repressive instruments, was decapitated and like the hot coals on which cold water had been poured was shrinking and dying. *Kitfuv Mboo* was a counter force, the spirit of a new beginning, indeed a new man under the rays of the sun. It symbolised the rising sun and nothing but the people's victory itself. The transformation was not only in dance and music. **Kitfuv Mboo** had a great impact even on older dances such as **Mndong, Njuh, Nfuh, Samba, Bimbo, Toh, Mbaya, Mbanglum,** among others.

In the field of arts, weaving; painting even agriculture, there was a change for the better. The Fakulum individually and collectively were determined to be their- own redeemer. The spirit of duty consciousness, nationalism and patriotism was overwhelming. A new sun shun on Fakulum in various ways which no force could extinguish.

The transformational impact of **Kitfuv Mboo** knew no barrier. Youths danced while running, jugging, or performing other acrobatic displays. In the church certain stereotypes which yesterday were taken as given were being questioned.

Lumnchu after attending doctrinal classes received baptism but refused to take a Christian name which he described as foreign and meaningless to him. The Rev.Father John Mark invited him for counselling for this was unprecedented in the life of the church in Africa.

'Lumnchu, you see, to demonstrate to the world that you have repented and turned away from the evil things of this sinful world, you must change your name and take a Christian name. I don't even know how to pronounce your name well either. A name such as Solomon in honour of the great king of the bible fits you well,' said the Rev. Fr. John Mark.

Fr., I appreciate your explanation. But tell me; is it my name Lumnchu that made me a sinner? Lumnchu asked, the Fr.

'No! Certainly not! But there is the issue of original sin which all mankind inherited from Adam and Eve. Added to this you, committed other sins.' said the Rev. Fr.

'By all mankind, this includes all human races, namely, blacks, Arabs, whites, Chinese, Indians, among others.' Lumnchu opined.

'Yes.' Said Fr. Mark, grinning uneasily.

'If, as declared by the holy scriptures, all have sinned and come short of the glory of God, and the original sin started with Adam and Eve, respectively father and mother of all humankind, how came it that one race, the white race, produced Christian names for other races? Is it not true that all names are cultural names? If some names are superior, with a universal appeal, then the culture that produced the names must equally be superior, isn't it?' Lumnchu questioned.

Rev. Fr. Mark was getting uneasy and regretting what pushed him into this discussion. But Lumnchu was not the type to be brushed off with the back of the hand. He knew from where he was coming and where he was going.

'Christian names are those found in the bible and we know what these great servants of the Lord did which each new Christian should follow the good example. And that is why I proposed the name 'Solomon' for you.' said Fr. Mark.

'Yes, Fr. I understand your explanation' he said respectfully. 'But as you have admitted, if a Christian name by itself will not qualify me for heaven, only faith will, so will my Nyamngong name, Lumnchu, not take me to hell. If it is my unbelief that can make me hell fire, then my Nyamngong name, Lumnchu can't block me from inhabiting a mansion in heaven. Angel Gabriel should find no difficulty in pronouncing my name let alone in writing it in the book of life.' Lumnchu said with such deserving finality that the Rev Fr. could not dispute.

Rev. Fr. Mark sensed that continuing with the discussion was going to belittle him before Lumnchu whom as a good singer they had been building a lot of hope in him. So he

159

thanked Lumnchu for coming and fixed a date to continue the discussion.' And they dispersed. But while Rev. Fr. Mark saw this postponement as an escape valve, Lumnchu was anxious for he still had much for the white man of God whose people tainted Christianity with their culture and wanted to impose on others.

Lumnchu was such a gifted artist that he was an asset to the church and choir. He was loved and admired by all both in church and in all of Nyamngong for his talents. He was an all-rounder. In church after listening to a sermon, he could just compose a song and as a song-giver stand and teach a new song which added meaning to the sermon and made people to understand the message even better. Rev. Fr. Mark had every good reason to handle Lumnchu with care for any effort to ridicule him could have a devastating boomerang effect.

At college, there was the study about the great men of God from the bible. The character this time around was King Solomon, who was exceptionally blessed with wealth and wisdom.

Rev. Fr. Anthony, the Principal was giving the lesson. And as every lesson ends with an interactive session within which questions are welcome, the Principal asked, 'Has any one a question or a comment?'

There were many hands raised up. Bantar was given the floor. 'Sir was King Solomon an African or a European king?' he asked.

Embarrassed, Fr. Anthony asked,' what does it matter whether he was a white or a black man?'

'Sir, it matters because we have never studied anything from the bible about an African. And you have always presented Africa as a dark continent inhabited by the heathen or pagans needing salvation. Secondly you have always presented polygamy as African and a sin. Nevertheless here is

King Solomon not only with so many wives but also many concubines yet was loved and blessed beyond description by God. In Nyamngong, HRH the Nyamndom has many wives, though nothing compared with King Solomon, it is a taboo for him to have a concubine, fidelity with his wives is a principle he cannot breach,' Bantar ended receiving whispering approval from his class mates.

Fr. Anthony looking askance had to tune his sixth sense before knowing how to handle the situation. His face had suddenly turned reddish. After some cool reflection he saw that anger against Bantar or punishment for asking such an embarrassing question could result in students uprising against his administration. Tactical handling was the only way out.

'Bantar, thank you! Your question needs an answer. But the few minutes remaining will not allow us adequate time to exhaust the question. Next time we will handle it before going into the new topic.'

Without waiting for the Principal to completely step out, everyone rushed to congratulate Bantar with a hand shake.

But as the Principal left the class, the question refused to leave him concentrate on other matters. It became a psychological torment. His mind told him that what was happening even in church and about Christian doctrine had something serious to do with the anger of the people against colonial rule. Within the missions it is whites dominating and the colonial rule it is same. Are these Africans beginning to see racism in the church so their anger against colonialism is having a spill over effect? He thought to himself and planned to consult other missionaries on the matter. It had never been like this for all my years of being here and in other African territories, he admonished himself.

Chapter Eighteen

My Pledge

My father though you are gone
And in my physical eyes
I see you no more
My mind's eyes are not blind
My mind's ears hear you loud and clear
You live in me for real

They say you died
That the Whiteman killed you
To forever reign and rule over us
To me you are not dead
You live in the spirit waxing strong
Those who die and are dead
Are the evil doers, traitors.

But you Ta Nformi Birr
My beloved father, the people's hope
You lived for a greater Fakulum
Those you have left behind
Confess you were their inspiration
Hope and pride for a new sun rise

Though you're now physically departed
Your disciples multiply by the day
For unquenchable is the seed of freedom
As ordained by the Creator Nyu-Ngong
You whole heartedly nurtured in the people
And they embraced will surely bloom and blossom

Your stand for human equality, freedom, dignity
Is the reality, making man, the natural man!
For you colonial rule is not determined by
Colour of the skin, be it white, yellow or black
But deprivation, exclusion, exploitation, subjugation
Talk of freedom, democracy, justice, peace, dignity,
development
Under foreign rule is pure sweet talk and fantasy
Alien domination and foreign rule is a declaration
Of war on the victim people and their land
 For prestige and grandeur of the foreign aggressor.

This you could not compromise
And for your people's freedom and dignity
You paid the supreme price and for this
You live in their consciences and spirit for real
And for this, truth and justice will triumph
And in freedom song Fakulum will gallantly rise to
In unity and solidarity match to greatness and fame
For alien rule is evil and will never triumph in perpetuity.

Standing here by the banks of Nyamngai
Facing Merri's encircled sand doom
Where Tatah Ngoh, your father who
With a drink to quench their tastes
Tricked sweet toothed invaders to eternal sleep
And facing Rtu Kaah across the Nsaah plain
I pledge never to compromise
With the enemy of our people, and our land.

For there's no nobler life
Than life lived in service
For greater humanity and justice

Ta Nformi Birr, you are not only an icon
By birth, but by your noble character
By your deeds, to redeem your people
And place them on Nyu Ngong's pathways
To drink deep to their fill from
Nature's refreshing and fulfilling glorious fountain
Of freedom, social justice, peace and prosperity.

Physical monuments of human minds and deceit
May like the Bismarck Fountain stand conspicuous
But they're symbols of imperial rule and bondage
To us they are meaningless chaffs of deceit
For Bismarck were neither us nor our hero.
Nor the Fountain a reflection of whom we are
Rather it's a stain to our psyche, history and culture.

As the Bismarck Fountain underscored our subjugation
So does this new caricature monument
A representation and symbol of foreign rule
And continuous dehumanisation, indeed neo-apartheid
And slavery of body, soul and mind
Of our people from cradle to the grave.

Like the Bismark Fountain on the toes of Mount Fako
The lackeys peddled to the colonial thrones
To please their mentors and glorify colonial rule
May rise to build a monument
In honour of General Pierre and other imperialists
But these all constructs of imperial minds and hands
Symbols of our enslavement and domination
Shall be reduced to shreds of nothingness
By the mighty axe of freedom and equal humanity

But your monument built of human love
For whom you are to your people
Lives in eternal history and culture
In songs, dances, arts of your people
You aren't dead, you belong to the ages.
And stand tall for a new humanity.

Yes! The torch of freedom and dignity
You lit in the people lives and burns on bright
Inspiring people to work for their redemption
The cry of freedom and self-determination unstoppable
For the corroding effects of alien rule are colour blind
And merit no sympathy from the colonised.

Ta Nformi Birr, my father
This is not only my pledge
As if I see you not, hear you not
I, Njemucharr, the living symbol and
The first seed of your manhood,
The blood of your blood
And spirit of your human spirit
Commune with you in the spiritual realm
And consciousness of the living.

Nyu-Ngong, the Supreme God ordained
That this land and all that abounds belongs
To no other people but the natives of the land
And that no other god shall share your glory
But you and you alone, Nyu-Ngong
Who ordained this land our blessed heritage!
And that to compromise and surrender to foreign rule
Shall be a desecration of the land and your honour.
For only a warm blooded son of the soil

Freely chosen by the people shall
As steward preside over the commonweal
According to the will and believes of the people

Yes, I pledge to remain faithful to your will
That as you lived a shared life for your people
I pray for wisdom and Nyu Ngong's spirit-filled life
That I never turn back on this fulfilling mission
To put a smile on every face and give hope to all
Fakulum shall be free; shall be free indeed!

Chapter Nineteen

News went all over that H.E. the President and Head of State was making his maiden visit to the historic port city of Covtoria. There was great excitement and serious mobilisation. Though there was excitement among the highly placed, there was however apprehension and feeling of indifference in the down trodden.

Principals of colleges and Head teachers of schools were instructed to mobilise and give the Head of State a befitting welcome. Traditional Rulers and the elites had specific roles in mobilising cultural groups for cultural manifestations and dances to demonstrate the loyalty of the people to the new found lord.

While those installed saw the maiden visit in bright colours and as face saving, the wretched of the earth compelled to turn out massively had reason not to be elated. To protect and preserve their positions the lackeys mounted pressure on the brow beaten Chiefs and the dregs of the society living on conscience money to ensure massive turn out of the population. As for those indifferent to the make belief, they were there for curiosity sake or what they call eye-shopping. The scars and traumatising experiences of the states of emergency were so strong and made them to have no faith in whatever thing was happening in the land for it was a counter to their legitimate aspirations.

Strongly opposed to an independent Fakulum the colonial master had withdrawn to the background and with the colonial lord of Frangoula fabricated a union of incompatibles between the two territories. To make things worse for Fakulum, the colonial master was more interested in replaying Pontius Pilate than affecting any meaningful union. While Frangoula was comfortably supported by HOME, Fakulum was a very healthy and beautiful baby left at the mercy of HOME and Frangoula.

As the population gathered at the ceremonial ground, the first to arrive were trucks filled with armed troops. This only reminded the people of the saga of the state of emergency under which they had been living for more than a year. With everything strange the troops speaking a strange language and not knowing by what names the two kinds were called – the population judging by their inhuman behaviour gave their own names. Those in brown khaki and red caps were called 'Mbere' and those in dark khaki and blue caps were called 'Kutuh'. The disgusting thing about them all was that they all looked unfriendly, fierce, aggressive and condescending. It looked as if they hardly smiled, let alone laugh. Their presence made the atmosphere turn chilly. The Nyamngong in general are intolerant of such haughty characters.

Soon a man arrived in a big vehicle fitted with huge loud speakers. He spoke a kind of Pidgin English with a strange heavy ascent that made it difficult for many to understand. Indeed he was a terrible forerunner who instead of making the path smooth and easy assured the anxious crowd of difficult days ahead. He filled the anxious hearts with doubts and apprehension.

From the blaring noise from the huge loud speakers the little that filtered into their ears and meaning drawn from was;

'Vwe na hear or vwe na no hear, vwe na kilap, vwe na kilap, vwe na kilap nnda so! Vwe na hear or vwe na no hear, vwe na kilap, vwe na kilap, vwe na kilap nnda so!!'

As the Presidential motor cade appeared from the hill descending to the field where the population gathered, the buffoon screamed the more as if to be heard by the master for a special recognition and award;

'Vwe na kilap! Vwe na kilap! Vwe na no hear, vwe na kilap! Vwe na kilap nnda so! Vwe na kilap!'

As the cheering started with those who first clasped their eyes on the Presidential motor cade and rose to a crescendo, teachers were having a hard time controlling their pupils and students as all were surging forward to have a glimpse of the President they had been given, had heard of and had come to see.

In responding to the welcome speeches the President had to speak through an interpreter. The interpreter himself a non Nyamngong, was not anything much better. He could neither speak Lingong which the absolute majority understood nor could he speak good fluent Pidgin English the lingua franca in Fakulum. As if to compensate for this irredeemable problem of communication, the buffoon seized the opportunity to scream through his exceptionally loud speakers 'vwe na kilap!, vwe na kilap! Vwe na kilap!' This drowned the poor interpretation and the unbearable grumblings from the crowd that this inevitably generated.

This only justified renewed debates as to what independence is and what it is not. The debate was intensive, among all social stratum of the society, the women, the men, the old and the young, most especially the students all over Fakulum. The unschooled were not left out of the debate either for the confusion was wild and telling. It was as if fuel had been added to blazing fire at noon under the hot tropical sun shine.

'I telli we na sa this talk sa white man don go, me I no know. Yes, I no belif. Say we don tanap by we sep. Wu sai we dey now?

'My broda lef me. We sabi dis man weh we di call sa na we Presiden? No be I hear sa when pipu tanab fo dem sep, na dem de chos dem presiden! Buk pipu call sa weti? Yes, sa na dem de vote dia Presiden? Wich day we fo dis we country vote yi?

171

Yi sep-sep sabi we? Yi no sabi we as we too no sabi yi.Yi be we contri man? Eh teli me!'

'So how yi cam be we Presiden? O na whiti man we i comot fo here go put yi for chai?

'I say massa, yu bi mbutuku? Yu sabi only for drin mimbu? Yu no hear sa dis one na join-join independen?'

Join-join independen na wich one? Some independen be black and someone be white or red?

In Club 54 some five members with matters of national interest uppermost in their minds had retired for a drink and to relax by playing some indoor games after yesterday's buffoonery. Club 54 initially was called Senior Service Club. Founded by the white colonialists, it was initially an exclusive preserve of the whites. This was when no black was a senior staff. But with attainment of self-government in 1954 and increasing number of graduates from secondary schools and universities abroad joining the civil service and managerial positions in government corporations at senior staff levels, there was evident and justified need for renewed christening of the Club. Seeing self-government as a historic and remarkable evidence of political development, the name Senior Staff Club, a sad reminder of yesteryear racism and white supremacy was changed to Club 54. This was the application of government policy of indigenisation both in government and in all social life, a demonstrable evidence of the people's determination to shape their destiny in conformity with their legitimate aspirations. It was living the Fakulum way or life style in defence of self- worth and identity. It was a mark of self-assertiveness and match to sovereign independence.

But as these five bosom friends got into Club 54 the enthusiasm for which ever game was not there at all. The burden bone out of the experiences of yesterday was so mind bungling that their nerves and minds could not concentrate.

Their spirits were so shattered and bodies on the other hand so broken that there could be no strength for any game.

'Let us be serious. I say very serious. Our independence has been postponed. What did you gather from the speech of the President yesterday? I said we have been trapped by this independence by joining. Is it not a serious contradiction that even with your level education you cannot even have a private discussion with your leader? He must bring in an interpreter?'

'You make me laugh, haha, haha, ha ha! Someone who does not know you and you are here dreaming and complaining of how will you have a private discussion with your dear head of state. Did you elect him to that chair? If not why should he bother about you?'

'And you qualify that just as a mere serious contradiction? It is more than that. My brother, it is far more than that. I qualify it as betrayal of a people. Yes, a total sell out! When the destiny of a people, their country and posterity is auctioned, you call it contradiction? You are kidding.'

'But he earlier said that our independence has been postponed. Why take it hard on him as if he is responsible? What is important now is to turn search lights on the problem to diagnose and seek a solution in conformity with truth, legality and our legitimate aspirations.'

'You are right. But you need understand why I qualify it betrayal. Now look around in South America, the Pacific countries, Africa, etc. where colonies and trust territories existed and tell me which country attained independence by joining. Among the troops, the Mbere and the Kutuh, were any our children? On which day did we elect that President?'

'You are talking of electing him; do we know the system in their country? Do we know whether he was appointed by the retreating colonial master as he has been imposed on us? Does he look like a democrat? If he were one, would he have accepted to be president over a people and a country he knows not? No democrat will accept such a thing. He is an agent to perpetuate colonial rule over us for the glory of his masters. Without external backing, on his own would he have been riding high over us?'

'Very true! Very, very true for democracy should be a way of national life for a people who are democrats. Democratic culture should influence and condition the totality of life, way of and order of doing things at the individual level and national level. In this regard, no one acts solely on personal interest and gains. What you do must have a positive impact on the other citizen and the society or nation at large. Democracy works for the flowering of the 'we identity first' and collective interest as against the 'my interest first.' The blossoming of a democratic culture is a bulwark against clique authoritarianism and dictatorship.'

'To me I see no difference between this and the Governor General, who left our country. The only difference is that this one is an African and the former was a white man.'

'But you perfectly understood the Governor General. You did not need an interpreter. Ndungu was an interpreter for the illiterate masses and not for Sasse boys and Oxford graduates as we all bowed in awkward humiliation yesterday. Tell me, was there any difference between you and the old mama farmer who does not know what the four walls of a classroom look like? So Joe, yesterday you were levelled down to an illiterate. You were deflated. And are still deflated today and who knows tomorrow!'

'Speaking seriously what I went through yesterday was too traumatising to call. It was a public disgrace to the intellectuals of this country. It was not only a national disgrace, it was an international disgrace. How do I tell my fellow Africans in Kenya, Ghana, Nigeria, you name it, with whom I was in

Oxford University that I needed an interpreter to pick some pieces from what my 'President' in quotes' he said it demonstrating with his two index fingers in the air, 'on a maiden visit said? You took note of how fiercely aggressive the mberes and the kutuhs were, pushing us as if we were miscreants!'

'Last year while attending a 'Conference on African Independence and South-South Cooperation' we were all moved by Dr Kwame Nkrumah's speech. How do you explain it that in Ghana I had no problems understanding the Ghanaian President as it was when I was studying in the UK. But in my own country I have to suffer what I would suffer in France or any of its former colonies? Oh, how disgusting and humiliating!' and he held his head in his two hands shaking lamentably from side to side.

'Joe, you have over looked one salient point.'

'And that is?'

'If your Kenyan or Ghanaian colleague were to ask you how you came about voting a foreigner, whose language you don't understand, to be you president, what answer will you give?'

'That is devastating. You did not hear me say my president in quotes? Why add salt to injury? That is a sharp knife driven through my heart. The question mocks me and all my generation. Believe me you!'

'Please give me an answer. All these lamentations can't be understood by your Ghanaian or Kenyan friend. They know as was the case in their respective countries that any person who emerged as President of post-colonial African nation was firstly a native of the colony. Secondly he fought for the independence of his country. In Ghana, for example, Nkrumah went to prison for refusing to be silent in the face colonial misrule, domination and exploitation. So was it also

175

the case with Jomo Kenyatta in Kenya. At the end they were democratic elections and the winner was proclaimed the Prime Minister or President. How is it that your own case seems to have been completely out of the way, in a class of its own?'

'That is exactly where the problem is. In the case of my country, all norms, all international instruments and conventions were set aside. It is sad, really sad.

'Indeed democracy demands that the people of any given territory defined by treaties under laws duly adopted by their representatives in parliament or by the people by way of popular referendum elect their leader from among themselves who will be answerable to them. Democracy makes it clear that the people are sovereign and the elected leader is custodian of the common weal. Under a democratic state everyone is under the law and the law makes state institutions strong and respect and enforcement of the law compulsory.

'Ok! There you are! So how do you recognise someone as your president whom you and your people did not vote for? Do you know the laws which brought him to power? How do you recognise him as your President when he was elected by people of a different country, people with whom you share nothing in common, be it language, culture, history, political system, same territory defined by inherited colonial treaties, or a common legal system?'

'But Ben, tell me, how did this issue of independence by joining come about?'

'To me that is not the issue for now! A wrong is a wrong! Independence by joining which imposed hurdles on our leaders and our people were led to the unholy altar like sacrificial lamb was completely illegal. It is a calamity that descended on a people like a plague. That is how bad it is! However yours is a question for historians and researchers. But that is not relevant for now. Life is a practical issue. It is not theory. You have had just one taste of it and you have come back from the field not only saddened; you are decapitated, you can neither eat nor drink. Put your -self into the future and see what our country, Fakulum, will be if things don't change now for the better. Is this the legacy we have to pass unto our innocent children? Do you know that by this treacherous act Fakulum will, like Carthage of old, disappear from the map of Africa? When Fakulum disappears, what becomes of its people? Assimilated and subjugated, right?'

'Yes, we can't recreate the past. But we can create the future. To do this we must understand what went wrong and from where we are coming and what we must do to shape a better future. We must identify the pit falls of yesterday and in patriotism and diligently work to avoid them. We have no right, whatsoever, to betray the future generation by burying the innocent into slavery. They have done no wrong to us and we should commit no wrong against them. This is no mean task. It is a national duty for patriots and visionary leaders. Our nation is not bereft of such a calibre of leaders. We must right the wrong, period,' and he hit the table so hard with his clenched fist that it attracted the attention others at the far end that were playing darts.

'Do you remember the buffoon who was screaming that people should clap and clap whether they understood what His Excellency said or not? Does he say that in his country? He took us for fools?'

'Do you blame him? And did some of our people not clap and clap? He does not need to say that in their country because the people and their leader speak the same language, know themselves. But this was not the case here.'

'You see that buffoon was charging and urging the population to clap and clap because he knew the importance of language in communication. Language has a cementing force. It draws and binds people together. Had the people not clapped and clapped as they did, non-clapping for not understanding would have amounted to a declaration of rejection, we do not know you. You are not one of us. We do not recognise you as our President. You are a stranger and you are President of a foreign country. None clapping would have graphically emphasised the dichotomy between our country and theirs, us and them. This should have sent home the strong message, we are not one, we are two distinct nations and peoples entitled to exclusive sovereign statehood and independent existence.'

'That is to say…'

'Yes, that is to say the buffoon played on our psyche. He played a strategic role by creating a false image of acceptance, 'Welcome our leader, our President.' The loud clapping that heralded his arrival created an atmosphere of conviviality. The clapping was needed to drown the tense atmosphere created by the absence of no link historically and culturally between the President and the population. None clapping would have painted the graphic picture 'There is no inclusivity. The President and his team belong apart. They are strangers visiting our country. There is no denying the fact.'

'Don't forget the fact that he came with some foreign Journalists and technical advisers from his colonial master. Those foreign experts have a special role to play. They were sent here to observe and give on the spot account of what the new acquisition looks like and how the natives received the new boss given them.'

'That is to say the buffoon was playing make belief!'

'Yes, of course he was. That is why he came ahead to measure the temperature and prepare the grounds. This also explains why he kept on driving round the field screaming, 'Vwe na kilap!, vwe na kilap! Vwe na hear or vwe na no hear,

178

vwe na kilap nnda so! In their interest, he was drumming support. In whichever way we look at it, how ill at ease some of us were at the field, his buffoonery worked perfectly well for his master and the international conspiracy against us and our country. With what passed for acceptance, their favourable reports have been written and dispatched HOME.'

'Comrade, as you rightly observed and as our discussion here has registered, this conspiracy code named 'independence by joining' has not only postponed our freedom and independence, it has prolonged our subjugation to foreign domination and colonial rule. We are neither free no independent so long as we are ruled not from within and by one of us but from outside by someone we do not even know. No nation that has suffered prolonged colonial subjugation, cultural assimilation, cultural dilution, economic rape can be developed and attain greatness without ethical revolution. Before we embark on any serious action, what we started in Nyamngai when in college must be revisited with vigour and nationalistic patriotism. There must, as of absolute necessity, be serious political education and mental decolonisation. As a matter of urgency we should regroup with a focus.'

Chapter Twenty

I salute you and through you, your mothers, brothers and sisters with all my heart, my soul and my mind. Since l left you physically, I have not left you spiritually, morally, socially and intellectually. I monitor every move of yours. You represent my living spirit.

The brutal murder of my physical body did not in any where affect my spiritual being. It is the physical body which is matter and by the law of nature it is transient. To die is to transit to the great beyond.

Know that the type of life lived on earth, prepares you for the life hereafter. Bad life on earth, leads to bad life in the hereafter. Once you are rejected both by the ancestors, the spirits and the minor gods who kept record of your life here on earth, Nyu Ngong rejects you. The rejected ones become evil spirits and torment the living on earth. This accounts for the growth of evil on earth.

But good life on earth, leads to greater life in the great beyond. Great men are not born great. Great men are borne of hard work, dedication and commitment to the general good. Great men are those whose lives impact the lives of their communities, nations and humanity in general. Great men are those whose lives shine like the morning star to show people the way forward for their good, these are people by whose character standards are shaped, these are people whose character is like the polished diamond that sparkles. And know that before diamond shines and sparkles, it must go through trials and fire. Great men and women are people of noble character, a reference point for generations unborn. These are patriots and heroes whose names are written in gold in the hearts of men, culture and history of the nation and humanity in general.

This visit to you is purposeful. For the task and mission you have committed yourself to makes it imperative that you know certain facts. These facts should reveal to you who you are, your mission for the good and dignity of your people here on earth, the true state of things and why things are the way there are. You need understand, my son, that the laws of nature are infinite and govern all other laws, the physical and unphysical, the visible and invisible and the here and the hereafter. It is a clear understanding of this that should guide you and enable you to identify pitfalls in advance and to serve your people and lead them attain their legitimate aspirations and collective self-fulfilment, these pitfalls must be well identified and understood and avoided at all cost. Until you do this you cannot forge ahead and find an enduring solution to the problem plaguing our people and country.

After the physical life I live in the spirit. From this vantage position I better understand Nyu Ngong's will for man than I did before. To each people Nyu Ngong ordained their heritage, gave them their culture and from this they build their language, their history, their laws and institutions, their way of life, their values, their likes and dislikes. All these put together distinguishes one people from another. As this distinguishes one from the other, it establishes boundaries. These boundaries have to be respected both by those inside and people outside. This mutual respect and understanding is not a matter of doing a favour to the other, it is must in that by so doing you obey divine law and demonstrate your humanity and integrity as ordained by Nyu Ngong, the omniscient and omnipotent.

In my days the enemy, the coloniser was easily and simply identified by his colour, then his overbearing attitude towards us the owners of the land. But this is not the case in your era. This makes your task complex, more demanding, difficult but not impossible. With tact and unity of purpose you will lead Fakulum people to victory over the aggressor. Fear not for rebellion against tyranny to restore a people banished to obscurity, desolation and servitude to regain mastery over their ordained heritage and freedom and dignity is doing the Creator's will. For those who dominate and enslave others brutally violate divine law. This makes the freedom fighter the true defender of the will of Nyu Ngong. Nyu Ngong is Love, Truth and Justice and the source of human freedom, equality and dignity. He cannot abandon those who fear him and do his will to suffer in the hands of evil doers. Nyu Ngong is the source of goodness, happiness and wellbeing. That is why to each people He did not only give them their land, from His source of abundance Nyu Ngong endowed their land with natural resources and from above provides rain to water their crops and sun to warm the crops to grow for their wellbeing.

As racist imperialism and colonialism could not be domesticated or refurbished to be accommodated so is it with foreign domination and alien rule Fakulum is subjected to. In reality this is nothing but a prolongation of colonial rule that has changed colour and become far more repressive, exploitative and overbearing. Colour has got nothing to do with injustice, suppression, exclusion, exploitation, deprivation that reduces a people to serfs on their own land. This alien rule is deceptive for there is no colour line for those who are blind to the reality about the inherent character of colonialism. What has made this current domination and foreign rule worse is the added dimension of annexation and assimilation aimed at annihilating Fakulum and declaring the people extinct.

The negative effects of colonialism and alien rule are not determined by colour. These negative effects manifest in the imposed misery, cultural assimilation, population dilution, and the decapitation of the people physically, morally, socially and intellectually, the economic plunder of the territory to perpetuate foreign rule for the grandeur and prestige of the metropolitan power and people. Indeed nothing has changed nor will it change. On the contrary things will only grow from bad to worse.

Any country subjected to foreign rule and domination is colonised society. Be not deceived about what colonialism is. It is not colour. Such a society is steeped in social injustice, it is divided and bedevilled by contradictions and as power is concentrated in the hands of the aliens and used abusively, the culture of survival of the fittest is born. Survival instinct which induces the subjugated in misery to act and listen more to their lower animal instinct leads those with sweet teeth and weak spines to betray others to be in the good books of and find favour with the coloniser. To make this the culture, things are tightened and depravity and scarcity of everything become the reality for the subjugated while the masters live in abundance.

Instutionalised reign of impunity and mass poverty dehumanise the people to the point that those with heavy appetite, sweet teeth and weak spines betray their humanity. They come to submit and bow to survival instinct as the only way out. These are traitors.

The system of ruler ship excludes those side-lined and the subjugated. These are the disenfranchised. Citizenship and unity should not be determined by political slogans. Citizenship is an inherent right by birth. It should never be measured by the opportunity given you to cast a ballot paper thrust into your hands by the ruling class. If you are granted the right to vote the elect or members of the ruling class to occupy positions of absolute power and influence and you are barred from such positions, it is clear you do not belong. Such a society is divided, a kind of cast society. It is a society of equals and unequal and the people belong unequally. While the equals or the elect, enjoy all rights, make and unmake, the unequal are excluded and subjected to the dictates of the equal who wield and control political, economic, military and judicial power exclusively. They are the holier than thou.

To maintain the established status quo those at the bottom of the society are brainwashed with half-baked truths. Falsehood and lies are made their religion dished out to them by the official media as freedom of the press is gagged. And once the mind is enslaved, mental decolonisation is the first approach to emancipation. My son, no one should deceive you about elections in structured society of equals, on the one hand, and the unequal, on the other hand, a society of the upper class and the lower class, rulers and the ruled. In a society of unequal, elections are used to confirm the established autocracy. In your case this autocratic rule is fortified by their mentors and the tyranny of numbers which you cannot upset. As for mentors you have none. But he who is on the side of truth, for justice sake and with Nyu Ngong is with the absolute majority.

My son, Njemucharr, I am talking to you from the great beyond for I have heard and seen the intolerable evil taking place in Fakulum. You are indeed popular. You have a great programme. The campaign team around you is great and has the capacity to do a good job. At the end you will win but because you are from Fakulum and since Fakulum is excluded from the ruling class, your attempt to upset the establishment will be intolerable and unacceptable. To the equal, your attempt will be viewed as rebellion against the established status quo, an act which must be crushed with al force. This may bring untold reign of impunities on a people who have suffered so unjustly for too long.

My son, listen to my instructions as you used to when you were young. The person controlling the process belongs to the ruling class. Members of the ruling class do not speak the ordinary language of the common people. They speak a different language which they alone understand. They work on oath. Autocrats make the laws and apply them autocratically according to their whims and caprices not general interest. Truth, honesty, fairness, justice, morality, among others, does not constitute part of their vocabulary. Not to talk less of the fear of Nyu Ngong. From their mannerism and what they say publicly and privately, I do not know if they know and believe in the existence of the Supreme Being, Nyu Ngong either. What pre-occupies them is self-interest and defence of clique interest. The ruling class has poisoned the minds of their ordinary folks against Fakulum. And their ordinary folks do this to continue to benefit from the crumbs that fall from the master's table. I have told you, everything is self-interest. There is no common weal.

If you were to win the contest, because you are an unequal, your name will not even be mentioned, let alone will you be declared the winner. Do they even want you to contest? You are not them and they are not you. Chickens of the hen and those of the bush fowl, though they may physically look alike, they do not feed together. Do not be misled by those surrounding you. Even ordinary humans maintain that what an elder sees sitting down the young at the top of the tree will not even see. Remember, I am talking to you from the great beyond. And I am standing on higher ground and I am imbued with spiritual insights. Above all I am dealing with spiritual forces.

Listen to me, my son. According to natural law, light and darkness do not cohabit let alone sleep on one bed. They live apart for they do not belong to one physical and spiritual realm.

You will not redeem the battered image of your people through this contest. Their salvation, political, cultural, spiritual, historical, economic, social, and even physical will not be attained through this contest.

And mind you, even animals and other lesser creatures, in respect of self- survival in dignity and defending inherent identity, know their territories which they defend. My son have you forgotten the lesson of the red and white cork in our house when you were still a lad?

'No! No! Father wait! Wait!' And he scampered out of deep sleep. It was then he discovered that he had been dreaming. 'So it was a dream, a real dream with my father? I saw him, real. It was the full life- size of my father standing by the door as if to block me from escaping until he was done. I heard him, fine and clear with his rumbling masculine deep voice when stressing a point. But when I opened my mouth to talk he vanished like a dark night twinkle little star.'

Njemucharr pitched on his bed for more than five minutes with his head in his two palms. 'What a dream so real?' he asked himself. In the dream he saw his father real and clear. Though it was almost two decade years, since his father was murdered in an anti-colonial war, Njemucharr had never had such a dream of his father. He prayed for forgiveness if he had gone astray.

Like a housefly he wiped his hands and face and prayed for sleep. He promised to reflect on the implications of the dream first thing in the morning. Considering the amount of work awaiting him in the morning, he badly needed some sound sleep.

As soon as he fell asleep, the father reappeared and the whole episode was replayed like the old grammar phone in which the conductor is requested to change the pin and play same record. He woke up dumfounded, perplexed and extremely weak. The dream had sapped the amount of energy in him away.

He stood between the deep sea and the devil. Should he give up and be called a coward? How could he explain the dream to his collaborators to be understood so that they appreciated his dilemma? The more he reflected, the more he was disturbed. But my father, whom I admire and adore, should I let him down because of those around me? How will he feel? How will those with who he is in the spirit world treat him? Will he still command their respect? Was the decision to talk to me in the dream his or he was sent by Nyu Ngong and the other spiritual forces?

But how could Nyu Ngong let me down or abandon me at this critical moment when I am doing his will? Once I am through the contest successfully I will enthrone justice and fairness and the unequal will be raised to equality. Then the truth, the infinite truth that Nyu Ngong created all men free and equal will reign eternally in the land.

Chapter Twenty One

The cream of those who mattered in the People Democratic Redemption Party (PDRP) gathered around Njemucharr. The purpose was to decide whether or not to go in for the contest. It was a critical decision to be taken for a critical moment in the life of a people. Njemucharr surveyed the circumstances and recalled the dream. In the context of the pressures from within and without he was like standing between the deep sea and the devil. The more he reflected on the issue, the more the love for his people bloom and his head ached from within. It was a trying moment in the life of a young man whose life was surrounded by mysteries.

'Yes we in the PDRP mean well for this nation. Judging from the philosophy of the PDRP and the party programme it is self-evident that the interest of the people counts first before that of the leader. There is no clique interest. The people are above the leader and not below the leader. The leader is responsible and accountable to the people and not vice versa. The ranks of our party are being filled by men, women and youths of all walks of life and from different parts of this country. But one thing is not very clear to me.'

'And what is that comrade?'

'Are we sure this contest will take place under open, free and fair circumstances? Are we sure PDRP with Njemucharr as its flag bearer will be allowed or accepted to contest?'

'Though I have never given thought to such questions, the seriousness and solemnity with which you pose the questions has set my mind wondering afield. I smell a rat. In fact I smell a rotten rat.'

'Whatever thing, comrades, that is why we are here gathered. The urgent issue is the registration of our party and the candidate. What we need know is, have the forms been filled and non-refundable fee paid as stipulated by the law?'

'The forms have been duly filled and certified. The required amount has been raised. But no treasury in this capital city, Mbarere, is ready to accept the amount and issue us the 'Special Clearance Certificate' (SCC). For the past four days we have moved from one Treasury to the other. The complaint is the same 'come later' or 'the officer in charge is not on seat.' In another Treasury we were told 'We are waiting for the SCC from the Ministry of Interior. The most frustrating thing is that those concerned treat us so disdainfully as if we were a nuisance. The way I see it, they are playing for time. Knowing that closing date is midnight after tomorrow, they want to apply structural elimination.'

'Comrades, must the money be paid only in a Treasury in the capital city? I think the law states in any Government Treasury within the national territory. Comrade Atem what makes you a slave to these holier than thou fellows who seize any opportunity to ridicule us? Move out from here and do what is desirable and doable.'

'And why should they apply such diabolic a measure against us? And what is this nonsense about structural elimination, if I may ask?'

'In a football competition when a team fails to turn up for the scheduled match, even if it were the team with the highest points on the score board, the team present wins by fore-feature. But here we see loyalists of the regime using delaying tactics so that we fail to register before the deadline. And once that is done, even if we complain in court, no one shall admit he ever saw us before giving one complain or the other. This is what I mean by structural elimination which is determined by in built hostility against a particular person or group to give undue advantage to a favoured candidate or group. Since the campaigns started, the ruling autocrats, their clan and mentors, seeing the massive turnouts at PDRP rallies are panic stricken. Consequently they will stop at nothing to apply this diabolic method of structural elimination.'

'With this brief explanation as to why PDRP and its leader have not yet been registered, you can see the relevance of my question.

'Remember the exceptionally huge rallies in Bakwa, Covtoria, Ladouma and Mbarere and the helicopters which like hawks floated in the air. What was the purpose? They took pictures of the crowds each time. Why? When we saw that, we self-congratulatory beat our chests and went to bed. We may have the large crowds at rallies; do we have the power to control the outcome of the contest? Do we control the in-built machinery? Have we forgotten that we are under a totally different system? Have we forgotten the souls murdered and those maimed in Bakwa the day PDRP was launched and the lies with which the public and international community at large were fed? Have we so soon forgotten that for the first time in human history and under the sun Priests, Imams, Magicians, Fortune Tellers, Bishops, Prophets, other Men of cassocks, Occult Priests, some flown in from abroad held an inter Ecumenical High Mass at the Cathedral of All Saints in Mbarere to pray against the foreign ideology imported by the PDRP and that PDRP and all its leaders should be swept away by an earth quake? Ladies and gentlemen, in all your life, have you ever seen or heard of such a strange combination of humans worshipping together in God's house? However that was a political holly mass held in the national capital with emphatically nothing spiritual to write home about.'

'But we have survived. All who prayed against and matched against our existence go around with tails in between their hind legs.'

'Who tells you? Their political pundits who use white lies and black lies to their credit as circumstances demand shamelessly preach that the high mass was specially organised to pray God to endow H. E. the Head of State with wisdom to grant democracy to our beloved country. As it is the government that gives freedom to the people, so does the government grant democracy to the country when the country is deemed mature for multiparty democracy. Consequently, according to them, those who were murdered by the forces and their agents working against the will of the people, died in vain.'

'Do they even accept that they killed and maimed peace loving and law abiding citizens? Their propaganda machine, audio-visual and print media churned it out that those who died were trampled upon. Could the physicians who saw the bullet ridden corpses and attended to the many wounded counter or testify? Comrade, this was just to fill in this important aspect! Complete your interesting analysis.'

'Thanks for that interesting point I would have left out. To conclude, it must be registered that the incontrovertible truth is that the blood of the souls murdered in cold blood in Bakwa sowed the seed of democracy and the PDRP brought democracy to this country. Having raised falsehood to a religion with H. E. as the high priest they claim credit for bringing democracy to this country forgetting the murdered souls, the political high mass and the numerous anti-democracy matches organised by those living on conscience money.

'With instruments of propaganda and all powers confiscated, the ruling oligarchy at will operates on make belief, today black is white and tomorrow white is black. Nothing happens but by the will and grace of the head of state. All ministers, judges of the courts, military commanders speak and swear by the name of the head of state.'

'With all due respect, what you have said is sound and logical but it does not address the issues raised. It is not a matter for emotions but profound reflections.'

'Let no one here misunderstand me. What do you mean by emotions? All that I have said is based on facts, verifiable facts. There should be no bite and blow game in the PDRP. We should be focused, face the bigger picture at all times. I am not opposed to our going in for the contest. Are we going in for the contest for its own sake? Or are we going in to please some quarters or because we believe in the system and that there will be a fair and transparent contest? What I want us to see and understand is the hurdles specifically put in place against us; not just PDRP as a party, not just Njemucharr as a candidate but us as a people and the democratic system for a better tomorrow for which we have already paid too great a price. We are committed to bringing democracy and to make democracy become a political way of life in this country. For a democratic culture to take roots in this country as it is, the PDRP needs to win and rule to transform the dictatorial institutions and constitution that have been in place since colonial rule.

'Take note, please take note, there are many contestants but why is it that only PDRP is facing difficulties of getting the SCC? Do not forget that it is our action through PDRP that has forced this type of contest onto the political landscape of this country. Democracy to them is mere theory. Multiparty democracy is strange and intolerable to them. Even the other contestants who pretend to be with us in the opposition are one foot in opposition and one foot with the ruling oligarchy. Why? They are self-seeking. On the other hand the few sincere ones among them confess our concept of freedom is too broad and strange to them. According to them, freedom comes from the government. This means the government dishes freedom to the few it likes and curtails or seizes even the little from whom it hates.'

'Yes, you have summed it up. Nothing illustrates the unbridgeable dichotomy between us and them than the fundamental issue of human freedom, equality and dignity and the rule of law. We have said it over and over that we belong apart. This explains why some are questioning the rational in participating in this election. What the common man, who at all times bears the greater burden, does not want is repeat of the mass suffering under the states of emergency.'

These disturbing challenges notwithstanding, after extensive to and fro debates for and against, it was finally unanimously agreed that PDRP must not run away from the animal just by seeing the horns. It was further agreed that any foul play will only prove the point of incompatibility of Fakulum and Frangoula being under one national state.

Secondly it was agreed that the PDRP whose well organized and coordinated campaigns have captured both national and international attention will become a laughing stock if it were to throw in the towel before the day of the contest. 'Let us go in for the contest and expose the hidden truth about the nature of things in this neo-colonial state and the character of the powers that have imposed hurdles for a fair and clean contest.'

This agreed Atem who had been charged with responsibility of registering and obtaining the SCC promised to do his utmost to accomplish the task even if it meant moving out of Mbarere. All prayed Nyu Ngong to guide him to success.

In addition to open rallies, printing of handbills, leaflets and placards propagating the ideology and plan of action of the

194

PDRP, door to door campaigns was introduced with determination to pursue this novel approach with vigour. The message of redemption, change and equal opportunity to all irrespective of social status swept throughout the national territory like the harmattan fire. All members of the old Friendship and Social Club (FSC) who were working within and without the country invested all their talents, resources and energy into wining more supporters for the PDRP. Kitfuv Mboo on the other hand was invigorated and carried the PDRP Flag high spreading the good news. This was unprecedented.

While Njemucharr and his populist PDRP were banking and counting on the support of the population, Jean Yande the incumbent president and the rest of the contestants groomed in the system relied on their colonial master who calls the final shot.

Two weeks to the 'D' Day, a special plane under tight security air-lifted all the candidates except Njemucharr HOME for final instructions. Among the instructions was a firm reminder about the Pact that was signed basis on which independence was granted. Ruler ship was made an exclusive preserve of and could only be entrusted into the hands of the faithful whose mind and heart were tuned towards HOME. It is such a person who adores the values of HOME that stability of the overseas young nation would be guaranteed by HOME. They were assured that the popularity of Njemucharr and his PDRP should tickle no one let alone give cause for concern. Results of the contest shall come from HOME in defence of the interest of the mother country and the umbilical cord relationship. No one would be favoured except he whose loyalty has been proven beyond doubt.

Within the two days of stay with their masters HOME His Excellency President Jean Yande was granted an interview on the forth coming political contest in his country.

'Your Excellency, you are few days away from a hotly contested election. Being the first in which you have a serious challenger, how is it that you feel so relaxed?'

'Thank you for your question. I feel so relaxed because I am confident of victory.'

'Your Excellency, how do you say you are confident when from turn out at rallies your challenger Njemucharr has recorded unprecedented huge turnouts? Your rallies, or those of your colleagues, if anything, are no match to his.'

'Firstly, your Njemucharr is a stranger; he speaks in a strange tongue so people go there out of curiosity. Secondly, he is a rabble arouser who attracts the loathsome fellows and those with idle minds. Thirdly you do not need to be carried away by crowds. Reality and power lies here and not there in those make-belief crowds. Finally, within the two days of our being here, my roots as the best pupil have been reaffirmed. How do you sacrifice the pupil you have nurtured for a purpose for an unknown stranger who will come and upset the entente cordiale? Of course remember the Pact!

'Your Excellency, permit me ask this last question. What is responsible for this cordial relationship between you and these other candidates here with you HOME and at this Press Conference? Isn't it strange?'

'Why should it be strange? We are together HOME because we belong to each other: we are brothers. We belong here. Each of us has a duty to defend and promote the Pacte our predecessor signed. I speak not for myself but for all the five of us. The consultation we had with H.E. the President and Patriarch went on well.'

'One more last question, Your Excellency, you talk of five of us. Why was the other candidate Njemucharr not invited?'

'He is an outsider. He does not belong. We were invited HOME to discuss family ties and secrets concerning HOME and our country in Africa. Should such involve a stranger? His country FAKULUM was never part of us when the Pacte was conceived and signed at HOME here. Do you expose family secretes to an unknown stranger?'

'Non!' came the chorus answer and they dispersed laughing at the programmed theatre contest.

Before the delegation was seen off they had last minutes discussions on 'Matters As Usual' with four key ministers, Foreign Affairs, Defence, Interior and Finance. Jean Yande was assured of victory in his favour. Time had not yet come for his replacement. The other four contestants were to be given juicy cabinet posts. More troops and special technical advisers to the Presidency, and Ministries of Foreign Affairs, Defence, Finance, and Interior that controls elections were to be dispatched to the territory immediately. This was to ensure that there was peace and stability as usual before, during and after the result of the contest were announced. Everything was to be as programmed, sealed and delivered. The public contest was to be a formality for the show of it.

Chapter Twenty-Two

Satisfied with success achieved HOME and with assurance from their mentors, the five contestants held a conclave on their return to adopt strategies for the days ahead, the D Day and beyond. The purpose of the conclave attended by the five and their top aids was to make a comprehensive evaluation of the outcome of the trip HOME, the situation on the ground and how to accomplish the mission firmly entrusted into their hands. The Conclave was presided over by His Excellency the President whose victory had already been guaranteed from HOME.

'Ladies and gentlemen, you are highly welcome to this meeting convened at short notice on our return. While some briefing by my colleagues at various party executive levels might have been done our sitting here together on the high table is self-evident that we are working together as one man for a clear defined purpose. Whether you believe it or not we are being challenged by an enemy inside the house. May be we had given him too much latitude. To put ourselves permanently on the driver's seat and put an end to the nuisance of challenge from the enemy inside, we must adopt strategies and with support from our mentors from HOME face the invader as one man. We must build a system in which we remain the master, calling the shots, and them the dregs of the society dancing to the music we dish out.

'As agreed HOME with our mentors, we cannot so soon forget the basis of our independence. To prove that our mentors and friends HOME remain our guardians more troops and technical experts will be arriving any time from today. As far as security is concerned before, during and after the contest, there should be no fear. We have the knife and the yam.' This was greeted with applauds.

'Thank you ladies and gentlemen. Let me give the floor to Hon. Alhadji Bouba Hassan. He should have something relevant to say before we go any further.'

'Thank you, Your Excellency for giving me the floor. Our trip HOME in the light of the task and strong ties between Mbarere and HOME, it should be agreed, was absolutely necessary and timely. In addition to the pledged support and agreements reached with investors for faster economic development, the meetings gave us an opportunity to strengthen the bonds of fraternity. We were also reminded of the north-south axil for the control of political power that was established at the dawn of our independence. We were seriously warned against being lured into communist sweet talk for the sake of change. Both our political and economic friends at HOME will see this as betrayal which will be resisted at all cost. Any such thing will ignite disaster. It is therefore in our interest to hold firm to what we know and avoid adventurism. Is it not said that a bird in hand is worth two in the bush?

'As a strategy, as agreed before our masters HOME, we the five political party leaders will maintain our respective political parties. We will continue the campaigns and each shall go in for the contest. But we already know the winner, H.E. here sitting.' And he turned respectfully with a gentle bow towards H.E. Jean Yande, on his right as all clapped approvingly. 'Our strategy' he continued, 'is to avoid the pendulum swinging out of control to the left. I believe you know what I mean by out of control to the left. The point is the status quo must be maintained. To tactfully do this, it demands new language; new concepts to make our people begin to distance themselves from the adventurer and to make him and his people know they do not belong. I learnt a new phrase 'son of the soil.' A 'son of the soil' has and enjoys all inherent rights and privileges. But this Njemucharr who is using his ***baton magique*** (magic stick) to pull large crowds to his rallies should be made to know that he is not a son of the soil. Above all our people should be made to know that he is not and as such cannot ascend the throne.'

'I fully agree with Hon Hassan and thank him for coming out so frankly and clearly. To make this very obvious the stick, the carrot and appropriate propaganda must be brought into full use. It is for this reason that the heads of strategic ministries, namely, Defence, Foreign Affairs, Finance, Interior, and Information and Propaganda and relevant heads of departments are here present. Particular attention is however expected of the Commander of the Armed Forces, the National Chief Security Officer and Minister for Information and Propaganda and his able National Director of Media and Broadcasting to the discussions and mapping out of strategies. Each has a strategic role to play and execution should be spotless and without error for desired result. We must prove to our mentors HOME that we are equal to the task. We must not let them down or betray the original agreement.'

'I sincerely salute His Excellency and Hon. Hassan for what each has said. Their presentations are so enlightening and inspiring.

'Let me make my small contribution. In addition to having the status quo and respecting the foundation on which this nation is built which we must defend, we must equally be mindful of the fact that this nation belongs to us. One big advantage that we seated here have which cannot be taken away from us is that we constitute the absolute majority of the population. Why should the majority surrender and be ruled by the minority? I therefore coin a new concept for use, 'majoritarianism'.

'This implies that the majority must of right rule and that the minority should respect the right of the majority to rule as of right. This is not a matter based on or to be decided by the ballot box. It is a given that we the majority should rule. In this context therefore, the minority should never attempt to nor should they ever be given the right to lord it over the majority. To allow such a situation it will tantamount to crowning a slave, king to rule over princes and princesses. This will be setting a dangerous precedence in the history of human kind.'

'Hon. Marie Blesse has spoken very well and I am happy with the new political concept which I know my Minister of Information and Propaganda like Goebbels will use his wits and with the able team expand and elaborate on it using all the instruments of the media to our advantage. Our rallies should regularly project heavy attendance. We work it out for people in PDRP uniform deserting and joining the ruling FPDU, men and women publicly tearing PDRP uniforms and party cards and declaring for the FPDU. The relevant authorities and departments know what to do to project this real. While the PDRP should be given a blackout, the FPDU should be given full coverage. The Radio Station and TV should open each time with a quote from His Excellency the President. The eye is the lamp of the human body and what it sees every time becomes the reality to the man, willingly or unwillingly. Njemucharr and his PDRP do not have these instruments of propaganda, so they cannot counter.'

'I thank you all for the bright ideas unfolding. Njemucharr is promising change. But he is an untested pilot. I am the embodiment of change! I have brought democracy. I have given freedom to the people. Without these two would he Njemucharr have been talking? But here he is not only biting the finger that has fed him, he wants to cut it. I have brought development and opened more schools. So what changes can an inexperienced and untested villager from Fakulum which we have absorbed into our geo-political entity Frangoula, bring to the people?' Amused at H.E's characterisation of Njemucharr as an untested villager from Fakulum, they all laughed as they clapped.

'Fakulum was not part of us at the foundation of this nation. Njemucharr and his people do not know from where we are coming and where we are going. The reins of power are in our hands and we remain accountable to the authorities HOME for what we do. Fakulum is not only a minority, it is absorbed and as stranger to an established system, they should watch, under study and take instructions. The sage advice that a fish caught in water, be it a stream or a pool, should never be washed in the very waters. It is washed and cleaned in different clean water. You make a mistake and wash it in the very waters; it will slip through your hands and disappear – fiap!' And he demonstrated with snapping of the thumb. All laughed including H.E. himself.

'Ladies and gentlemen I thank you, thank you that was just an appetiser to relax the brain. We are here for very serious business. The destiny of this nation lies in the outcome of this meeting and how we from hence stand together and cooperate with those who granted us independence. We the leaders lead and our people take from us and follow. We know the truth and the truth comes from above.

'This illustration about the fish explains what assimilation is all about. Why clean a caught fish in different water? The different water is not as fresh as the water from which the fish was caught. The different water is unknown to the fish but very familiar to the fisherman. On the other hand the fisherman does not want the fish remain alive, strong and with capacity to swim away. The assimilated have to be disempowered to facilitate annexation. Assimilation is to transform the assimilated from full citizens into sub humans. They must conform to new ways and be what we want them to be. When someone comes into your house you show him a seat. We have to make these petty Fakulum forget about their country and believe only in Frangoula. We must scrap from their minds and consciences their belief that Fakulum was ever a reality nor is it a reality and they a people with a culture, a history, a language and a civilisation thus with an inherent right to sovereignty and to shape their destiny. They must accept our culture, history, language, civilization and political system as the only reality in Frangoula and that Frangoula is one Frangoula. On the philosophy of catch them young, history and geography school books right from nursery to university have to be dusted and rewritten. For easy assimilation everything must be concentrated in our national capital, Mbarere.'

'Your Excellency, you have struck the nail on the head. And this pleases me greatly. I have always been worried about this noise of human freedom and equality. This is what has made Njemucharr to believe that he can rule this country. Good enough the fate of the small brat has been sealed at the source of our power. The equals compete with equals: equals do not compete with unequal. By our language and action, this must be made clear.

'To make the territory absorbed cease from being distinct we must encourage our citizens to populate that territory as much as possible. Population dilution must be an effective government policy of national integration and national unity. In theory and practical terms, this must mean uniformity and conformity. This reinforced by our citizens occupying strategic positions and dominating in administration, the economy and finance, the judiciary, armed forces, and security will expedite assimilation which is key to erasing them off. Identity must be backed by capacity to exist distinctively. This we must block.

204

'To disempower them and maintain them as the dregs of our beloved nation the politics of exclusion must not only be maintained, it should be intensified. Even the most loyal should be fit only for sinecure post, post of vice, assistant and deputy. The most loyal appointed to a sinecure post must be watched by one of us as his assistant. What Njemucharr has done and the euphoria his candidature created should serve as a serious eye opener to us all.'

'I welcome sincerely the laudable points, strong ingredients for new government policies proposed by Hon. Issa Toukour. In appreciation may I assure you all that we are already functioning here as the new government'. His Excellency's assurance received prolonged applauds.

'All what you have suggested comes under guided democracy. A solid foundation must be laid for the house to endure all challenges of bad weather. Njemucharr and his PDRP should not behave as if they have a monopoly of what democracy is. Guided democracy will strengthen the rights of the equal to rule as against the rights of the unequal to rule. It will equally guarantee that you never organise elections and be defeated. If so why sit on the driver's seat, with all the levers in your hands, organise an election only to be humiliated?

'On the other hand while at roof top we proclaim that all are equal, in practice the policy of exclusion will determine who is who and whose word matters in this land. Meritocracy has no place or it is as determined by the decision maker, who must be one of us. To keep them permanently under our thumb, scarcity and depravity must become their lot. In the civil service, judiciary, military, among others, meritocracy, qualification, experience, will be sacrificed on the altar of majoritarianism.

'And to keep them permanently submissive, worshipfully at our beck and call, make them miserably poor. While fighting poverty here as per the UN Millennium Development Goals, over there we reverse and fight the poor. To dismiss the idea of a past which they can look up to, what they had such as political, administrative, economic, socio-cultural and legal institutions, before being absorbed should be abolished while the affluent institutions are nationalized and transferred to our territory. Institutions that remind them of their distinct identity and which could give them nostalgic feelings and self-pride should not be allowed to survive or be maintained in their hands. The poor are voiceless, subservient, and powerless; they are gullible and easy to be manipulated.

'Consequently, the right of their children to education must be limited. So is it with right to employment... And the august assembly happily answered Limited!

'Right to promotion in the civil service, judiciary and army?'

'Limited!'

'Right to development in their part of the country?'

'Limited!'

'Right to industrialization in their part?'

'Limited!'

'And right to any of them to rule us?'

And they all shouted hitting their tables 'NEVER! NEVER!! NEVER!!!' Congratulating themselves with a full happy laughter. H. E. himself amused by this exercise put up an amazingly boyish smile from ear to ear in spite of his age.

Ladies and gentlemen, thank you very much. We are indeed on the move and on the right path of excellence for our people and to make our great nation united, indivisible and strong and to maintain it the oasis of peace and stability on the African continent. Some of the issues we have discussed and agreed upon here will be put into immediate effect by Presidential decree by tomorrow.

The conclave closed with a well-deserved banquet in the lavishly decorated Banquet Hall of the Presidential Palace. The tables were set with the best wines, champagnes and foods you could think of in any Palace under the sky. And of course, the damsels to serve were not only specially dressed for the occasion; they were well drilled. The deal was sealed so they had reason to celebrate!

As the days to the D Day narrowed down every party and every candidate intensified the campaigns. Certain things became so obvious. The PDRP suffered a kind of blackout on radio and television which were all owned by government. The FDPU and the government were just two sides of the same coin. The ruling party and other four parties that had members in parliament enjoyed excellent coverage. But the ruling party was regularly in the news.

The second noticeable thing was change of attitude in the other candidates. All the five candidates concentrated their attacks on Njemucharr and the PDRP. While projecting Njemucharr most negatively, the electorate was told a vote cast for Njemucharr and his PDRP was a vote in futility. Corruption and patronage became the order of the day. In Fakulum, the security like mad dogs was let loose after the harmless believers in democracy. While Njemucharr and his campaign teams were harassed and chased away in districts where the other five parties had an upper hand, PDRP leaders and supporters enjoyed no protection of any kind. They were at the beck and call of security officers who harassed, intimidated and even arrested and detained some leaders of campaign teams. In some areas, most especially in the President's home province, the populations declared their zone no go area for the PDRP. With free license to terrorise PDRP supporters, numbers at public rallies plummeted greatly. But the fire was kept blazing by the strategic door to door campaigns.

With the propaganda machine sharpened and make-belief at its best, the Presidential Candidate of the FPDU became a 'Man of the People', the People's Candidate,' the Ordained Candidate,' 'the Messiah of the Nation,' the Man of Peace and Development,' 'the God sent Leader,' 'the People's Choice,' among others. Flyers and large bill boards at strategic points all over the national territory and on radio and television carried all such slogans at the tax payers' expense. Such make belief was to justify the already concluded victory.

With heavy military and security presence the elections went on hitch free. But it was uneasy calm for the troops were armed to the teeth. The situation was worse in Fakulum, especially in Bakwa. But the people voted quietly and returned to their homes. The turnout in Fakulum was massive for the people, with their old faith in the power of the ballot box, were committed to change.

Five days preceding the proclamation of the results, the Minister of Information and Propaganda granted a Press Conference on the ever first multiparty democratic elections in the country. He said though it was the first ever in the country, he was proud to say that older democracies in the world such as USA, Britain, Canada, among others, had a lesson to learn from Frangoula. He congratulated the army, the security and the different political parties for guaranteeing peace, security and stability. He declared that H.E. the President, from more than 70% of the votes counted, was already enjoying absolute majority. This was a storming declaration!

'Sir, the electoral law forbids any one except the President of the Electoral Commission to declare any results, partial or fully. How do you as a minister violate the law?'

'Yes Mr. Journalist, I am aware of that. The Government makes the law. Mark you, what I have said even God cannot alter'.

Twenty one days after people went to the polls, the Electoral Commission President announced the results. The incumbent President H.E. Jean Yande was declared winner. This was contrary to popular expectations.

Night proceeding the declaration of the result, Bakwa, headquarters of the PDRP and hometown of Njemucharr the PDRP flag bearer, was subjected to greater troops reinforcement. It was once more receiving the baptism of fire under military siege. As planned act to ignite unrest for greater punishment on the population, there was massive arrest and torture of PDRP leaders and supporters. Troop reinforcement got involved in arson, looting, raping, maiming and killings under the pretext of maintaining calm and state authority. While this was the reality on the ground, the state media outfits were dishing out falsified information of how organized PDRP youth vandals had unleashed a reign of terror in Bakwa and other towns in Fakulum's two provinces after losing in an open and transparent democratic election carried out under peace and tranquillity. To ridicule Njemucharr the more, the other four candidates who performed worse than Njemucharr were congratulated for their sense of maturity and sportsmanship. The four candidates conceded defeat, congratulated H.E. the President and pledged their support and cooperation to move the nation forward.

To expose Njemucharr as a trouble shooter a three months state of emergency renewable was imposed in Fakulum. The clear winner of the Presidential election became the vanquished caged and rewarded with house arrest with set of armed troops ringed round his residence. Justifying the inhuman house arrest and imposed state of emergency, the

Minister of Interior described Njemucharr as '*l' enfant terrible*' who, lacking in democratic culture and spirit of sportsmanship was out to destabilise a peaceful nation all Africa looked up to as an oasis of peace and stability after he lost in a clean and transparent democratic election. His immediate lieutenants were either in maximum detention or on the run. This unprovoked attack on the leadership of the PDRP and isolation of its leader was to get to the roots of this party that had shaken the foundation of Frangoula. The atrocities that visited Fakulum and the attack on the leadership of PDRP were to disable it to the point that it would hardly ever regain its vitality, soul and spirit.

In isolation under house arrest Njemucharr took a retreat to his last confrontation with his father in the dream. He regretted harkening to popular pressures instead of the silent word of wisdom. 'Once you do not belong, the solution lies in investing in righting the errors and retreating to hold your own ground. You can never be a master in someone's house.'

Though alone isolated under house arrest with his key lieutenants under solitary confinements in most dreaded cells in the country or in hiding, he assured himself, it is a battle lost not the war against gruesome injustice of my people. Pepping into the future he saw twilight of hope.

'We must set on a new mission, the mission of reality, the mission of real politick, the mission of the people's freedom defined by our cultural heritage, history and territory. This contest has proven the incontestable, namely, that we do not belong. The fundamental question facing all Fakulum is 'Who are we? Who are not us? And who is against us?' Retreating to hold unto and defending what is yours by divine and international law in order to be who truly you are is what civilised man has stood for to shape the world for greater humanity,' he concluded.

Printed in the United States
By Bookmasters